"Johnny's narration, the clever plot twists, and lots of action pulled me into the story. When forced to defend his ma and himself, Johnny made hard choices, decisions that turned a teenager into a man. I hope to hear more from him. Will this be a series?" *Wanda Snow Porter, Author*

"The character development is so well done that it's as if Johnny was sitting in my living room telling the story. The plots and subplots are wonderful. I love the who's who that kept the suspense heightened. It's the best book I've read this year. Well done!" *Fiona – Editor for Readers' Favorite*

Other Titles by **R Lawson Gamble**

Zack Tolliver, FBI Series of Mysteries

THE DARK ROAD

THE OTHER

MESTACLOCAN

ZACA

CAT

UNDER DESERT SAND

CANAAN'S SECRET

LAS CRUCES

Johnny & The Kid
An Old Time Western

By R Lawson Gamble

My thanks to Craig, as always, for his usual meticulous and enthusiastic reading and to Wanda Snow Porter for her insights, comments, and "Horse Sense".

To Ma and Pa Gamble from their pistol-packin' little boy
"Two-Gun" Ricardo

CHAPTER ONE

He was alone among the men at the bar, just another thirsty cowboy until you noticed the way the other men left him space, not turning their backs on him or anything, just shaded away as if it didn't mean one thing or another. A shot glass sat on the bar in front of him, full and untouched, a present waiting to be opened. It held his eyes as if a special secret lurked in its dark depths. His left boot rested on the foot rail, his hands lay palm down on the slick mahogany bar either side of the glass, relaxed and easy.

He wasn't a big man. Most others at the bar were a head taller or broader in the shoulders. It wasn't the look of him you noticed right away, it was something about him you felt rather than saw that set him apart. To look at him, he wasn't paying attention to anything but that shot glass of whisky yet somehow you knew he was taking in everything going on around him.

I picked him out as soon as I came in the door even though his back was to me. It took a moment for my eyes to adjust to the dim light and then I saw him— slender, lithe, the black felt hat brown with trail dust, the back of a leather vest worn slick in places, his left leg up on the foot rail so the protruding walnut grip of his six gun cocked slightly away from his body, keeping it free. I'd heard he shot lefty.

The thing was, even paying no mind to everyone else in the room just standing there staring into that whisky glass, he gave you the feeling of a tiger ready to spring. No one looked his way, but you could tell everyone felt the same thing.

This was the man I had come to find. According to rumor he was with the Flying R cowboys bringing up a herd from south Texas. I'd come to see if it was true. I knew now it was.

"Now you just go see if he's there, Johnny," Ike had said. Ike Sanders was owner and editor of the Liberty News. He was an older man with brown leather cheeks and bushy eyebrows over blue eyes that usually twinkled. Right then, though, they didn't. "Don't you go trying to talk to him. Just go look and come back here and tell me if you seen him."

Well I was there, and I seen him, and I should have left right then. Maybe things would've been different if I'd done that. But I didn't. I just stood there and stared. I'd never seen a gunfighter before.

The card tables in the Lucky 7 Saloon were busy like they always were when trail drives came to town. Deep Water, Texas was a small place still hoping the railroads might drop a spur line south from Kansas. These days most outfits drove their cattle east of us up through Indian Territory to Abilene. But the big herds ate up the grasses and when that happened the outfit following behind sometimes swung west to look for more grass and so they come our way. That's when Deep Water turned from a few scattered buildings baking in the sun to bustling streets and singing cash registers. It's how the town got by.

When the cowboys came in, card sharks appeared out of whatever hole they'd been hiding in, hotel maids and waitresses transformed into glamour girls, and old Bill Spence, owner of the Lucky 7 Saloon hired up an extra shotgun guard and two more bartenders. Everyone came to town just to sniff the excitement in the air, try their luck at a big game, or just listen to the stories and brags of the cowboys who had been everywhere and done everything you wished you had done. It was a high old time for everyone. But we'd never had a bona fide gunfighter in town before. And there he was right in front of me staring into his drink.

"Why're you here, boy?"

The question came unexpected out of nowhere and hung in the suddenly still air. The gunfighter hadn't moved, his head hadn't turned but I knew he was the one spoke and he was talking to me.

His words weren't loud, they were soft and kind of easy going but the moment he said them every other conversation in the room stopped. Cards silenced mid-shuffle, drinks paused on the way to or from mouths. As loud as it was before he spoke, it was that quiet now.

It was me he was speaking to and he was waiting for an answer. He still hadn't moved, hadn't turned to look at me. But I knew he was talking to me and everyone else in the room knew it too. Everyone was waiting.

I couldn't say a word. I couldn't make my mouth work, didn't know what to say even if I could speak. I couldn't just say, "I came looking for you." I figured I'd be deader than dead before the words were even out of my mouth. So, like a fool, I just stood there, my mouth opening and closing like a lizard.

"Did Ike send you here, boy?"

Right when the question came, he turned to face me, so smooth and quick I might of missed it if I wasn't starin' at him. His eyes were on me in a snap and I knew if he'd wanted to pull his gun when he turned nobody in the world would've stood a chance, but instead he was just leaning there with his back against the bar and his thumbs hooked in his gun belt looking at me. Waiting.

His eyes were black as coal. I'd never seen eyes like that, deep and empty. His black hair curled out from under his hat. He looked Indian, his skin was shaded brown that way but seemed lighter, maybe because his eyes was so dark. His face was flat and still. That was how he looked to me.

My mouth wouldn't work but I could nod my head, so I did.

He just kept looking. Everybody was looking and waiting. Tobacco smoke hung hazy in the lights and the ceiling fan creaked on its chain. There was the smell of warm beer. A fly buzzed.

"You tell Ike I'm here."

I found out my legs worked just fine. The sunshine in the street never felt warmer or looked brighter. When I stumbled into the print shop Ike took one look at me and stopped work.

"Well?"

I was gasping. "He said to tell you he's here."

3

Ike nodded quiet-like as if he knew all along that would be the way of it. He sat me down and fetched me a glass of water. He gave me a long look.

"I need you to do one more thing. I need you to go back there and give him a message from me."

My heart starting pounding at the very thought. My hand shook so the water in the glass nearly spilled. "I don't think I can do that," I said.

He hunched down so he could look me right in the eye. His face was calm, his reassuring. "You can do it. You'll be all right."

I had a lot of respect for Ike, otherwise I'd never have gone back to that bar. When I was outside the saloon, I stood on the boardwalk and took a deep breath. Then I pushed the door open slow and stepped inside.

He was waiting there in the same place, leaning back against the bar, his thumbs hooked in his belt, staring at me. The place hushed as soon as I came in. Everyone turned to watch.

The black eyes stared. "Well?"

"He ain't comin'," I blurted.

The black eyes stared some more.

I stood there, quaking inside. Nothin' else I could say. That was the message.

"He'll come."

Snake-like quick, the gunfighter reached out a hand toward the cowboy nearest him. The next thing you know that cowboy's pistol was in the gunfighter's right hand, angled toward the floor.

The cowboy started to open his mouth, changed his mind and shut it.

The black eyes held onto mine. He leaned down and placed the pistol on the wood floor. When he rose back up, he kicked it. The gun skidded and slid across the floor and ended up at my feet.

"Pick it up."

My stomach clenched and my chest tightened to a knot. I shook my head.

"You don't pick it up I'll kill you anyway."

Sweat beaded out on my face, my palms were wet with it. I shook my head again. "I can't." It came out like a whisper. My fear was so strong everything around me seemed misty. All I could see was those black eyes. They showed nothing.

Another voice cut the silence, low pitched, calm. "You planning to shoot an unarmed boy?"

The black eyes stayed on me. "Hello, Ike. I been expecting you."

I wanted to look for Ike, but the gunfighter's eyes held me. Ike's voice sounded from somewhere behind the bar. He must have come in the back door.

"You ever know me to lie, Kid?" That was Ike's question.

"You don't lie, Ike."

"Then you'd best know I'm holding a twelve-gauge pointed at your back."

"You never were a back shooter, Ike."

"I am today, Kid."

The black eyes never left mine. "I can kill the boy before you can pull that trigger, old man."

"You'd still be dead."

5

"We can settle this out in the street. Leave your boy out of it."

"I'm weary of talking, Kid. Drop that gun belt using just your right hand moving real slow. If the other hand moves, you die."

The gunfighter did as he was told but those vacant black eyes stayed on me. He didn't hesitate or argue. His right hand crept to his belt, undid the buckle, let the belt and holster slide to the floor where it wrapped at his feet.

"Now kick it toward the boy."

He did.

"Johnny, pick up both guns."

To my surprise, I could move. As quick as I could I picked up the guns, holster and cartridge belt and clutched them all to my chest. Then I stepped back away.

The black eyes stayed on me. I felt like we had a rattlesnake in a pail without a lid.

Ike marched the gunfighter out through the saloon door, the shotgun at the man's back the whole way. I followed after him and the crowd came after me.

We all came out into the street like a funeral procession, Ike and the gunfighter leading, the shotgun between them. They stopped at a black stallion and Ike watched the gunman mount up.

After he climbed into his saddle, the gunfighter looked down at Ike. "I see you got my Winchester too, old man." Then he did something strange. He laughed. It was strange because it was the first time his face looked anything but blank. His eyes didn't laugh, though, just his mouth.

"You take good care of those weapons, old man," he said. "I'll be back for them."

6

He reined his horse around, spurred it and trotted down the street and out of town. He never looked back.

CHAPTER TWO

Ike Sanders came to Deep Water the year I turned ten. I don't remember anything special about his arrival. Men on horseback drifted in and out of town regularly. They all had the same look, dust covered and weary. They always rode straight to the Lucky 7 Saloon. Next day or two, they'd be gone. Wasn't much to keep them here.

The thing about Ike was he stayed. He stayed on account of my mother.

My dad was killed by a rattlesnake when I was small. I can hardly remember what he looked like except I can still see his arm black and swollen where he lay on the bed. Since there was no doctor close enough to do any good, an old Indian tried to cure him with plants and poultices but that wasn't enough. He died quiet, uncomplaining. He was a tough man.

There weren't many women in Deep Water and my ma was good looking and smart. Men came courting after my dad died but she said no to all of them. My dad was special, she always told me, and nobody she'd seen yet could match him. She took to mending clothing to get by and we kept up the goat herd. When the Lucky 7 Saloon got crowded Mr. Spence would sometimes pay her to wash glasses and wipe tables. That's where Ike saw her.

Ike didn't court her, but he noticed her. She mentioned him to me from time to time, about how he was always gentle around her and courteous. He lived in a room in the Lucky 7 and ate his meals at the bar. He didn't seem inclined to move on.

Ike appeared to have all the money he needed, and people noticed how he wasn't looking around for work even if there was any, which usually there wasn't. After a while, he became a fixture in town, and nobody thought much more about it. People liked him for his manners and his helpfulness. Mr. Spence was happy to have Ike around. He was always willing to lend a hand when things got crowded in the saloon.

I was twelve the year Ike up and bought the old Campbell store. It was just a one floor building, a bit shabby for having sat empty for years. Kids broke some of the windows with rocks, and saddle tramps slept on the floor. The dry Texas dust sifted in through cracks in the walls.

Ike didn't say why he bought the building, but he was in there every day fixing and cleaning and painting. When I passed by, I'd try to get a glimpse inside. I saw what looked like one big room with shelves and cubbyholes around the walls and lots of empty floor space.

It wasn't until the Wells Fargo wagon arrived with a large crate that needed six men to lift it out and carry it inside that word got around Ike had bought a printing press. It seemed like Deep Water was about to have a newspaper.

Soon after that Ike came to the house. He told us he intended to start up the Deep Water Liberty News, but he couldn't do it by himself. He needed a boy to work in the print shop and help deliver the newspapers. It would be an internship with pay that would grow as the newspaper grew. I thought it was a great idea.

Ma had questions. What made Mr. Sanders believe a small town like Deep Water needed or would even support a newspaper?

Ike told her the town would grow, maybe just because of the newspaper. "A newspaper in a town offers refinement," he said. "It says civilized, like a church or a school."

We didn't have those in Deep Water, either.

You could tell my ma was impressed. "What do you know about printing a newspaper?" was her next question.

Ike explained how he himself had been interned in a newspaper office as a boy but had turned to other things as a young man. Now he had a yearning to get back to it.

That's how I come to work for Ike Sanders at the office of the Deep Water Liberty News. He paid me a good starting wage, but I worked hard for it. There was a lot to do in those startup years. I often worked long hours and through the weekends.

Ike was right. The town did grow some and took on a certain air, maybe not of gentility but at least of self-importance. There wasn't enough kids yet for a school and not enough interest in starting a church. But there was always news, whether it was brought by strangers passing through or came from me talking to townspeople, like when Mrs. Cline's chickens weren't laying. I did a lot of stories on Mrs. Cline's chickens.

Townsfolk liked to contribute editorials to the paper from time to time, too. They liked to see their opinions in print.

I learned the newspaper trade just as Ike had promised. I began by sweeping the floor, cleaning type, and mixing ink from powder. I later learned to lever the press and advance copy. Ike did all the type setting, though. And he wrote all the stories.

We worked as a team gathering the news. Often people would stop me in the street and tell me what was happening. When a stranger came to town, Ike sent me to interview him and see if he had any news worth printing.

That's how I thought it would be when the gunfighter came to town. Instead here I was standing with my arms full of guns watching the last bit of dust settle at the far end of town. Most of the Flying R cowboys had gone right back to the bar but the townsfolk stayed. You could tell they was all busting to ask Ike questions.

Ike never turned to look at them. He walked straight on down the street to the newspaper office. I followed him. As soon as I was safe inside my knees turned wobbly and I went and sat down in the chair, still holding the guns and the holster belt. I watched Ike hang the shotgun up where he always kept it. Under it, leaning up against the wall was a Remington lever action rifle I'd never seen before.

Ike came over to where I sat and took the two guns and the holster belt from me. He put them down on the floor and pulled another chair up next to me.

"I'm sorry I put you in that position, Johnny. I didn't expect he'd do what he did to you."

"He wanted to kill me." My voice came out half whispering, half croaking.

"I would never have let that happen."

I wasn't so sure. I'd seen how quick that gunfighter could move. What if Ike had been a few minutes late coming in the back? What if the gunfighter had decided to try to kill us both even with a shotgun pointed at his back?

But I didn't say any of those things. I had other questions. "How do you know him? Why did he want you? How did he know it was you sent me there?"

Ike stood and stared down at me, his fingers holding his chin like he was deciding what he wanted to say. Then he sighed. "I need to talk this over with you and your mother together. You go home now, show her you're okay. People might already have told her about this. I'll come along soon as I give that cowboy's gun back to him."

It felt steadier when I stood up. "Will the gunfighter come back?"

Ike gave me a long look. "For sure, he'll be back. Not right away, though."

I walked home like Ike asked me to do and he was right. We lived about a half mile out of town, but Ma had already heard about what happened. She ran out of the house and grabbed hold of me hard. I could tell by the tenseness of her body she was real upset but all she did was hold me for a long while. Then she pulled me into the house and sat me down at the kitchen table. I looked around the warm, familiar room with the bright colored curtains, blue rimmed dinner plates on their stands, and all the little things Ma found to brighten the room.

"Thank god you are alright. You want some water or some hot tea?" She started for the stove.

R Lawson Gamble

When I shook my head, she sat down across from me and told me to tell her everything that happened and not leave anything out.

I did. As I told her I saw her eyes turn watery and I knew she was growing scared for me thinking how close it had been.

There was a knock on the door.

Ma knew who it was. "You come on in, Ike." Her voice was hard.

Ike came and stood by the table, his hat in both hands. I saw right away there was something different about him. He was standing in a different way, straighter, maybe. And he was wearing a gun. I'd never seen him wear one before, yet now it seemed part of him.

Ma didn't offer him a seat. He didn't look like he expected her to. She just stared at him and said, "Ike Sanders, who *are* you?"

Ike looked sorrowful. "You're right, ma'am. I'm not the man I've tried to be here in Deep Water. It has always been my belief a man could change himself if he wanted to bad enough. But there's nowhere to go to hide from the past. The past won't let go of a man."

Ma shook her head like she wanted to shake out everything she was hearing. "Mr. Sanders, you have been good to us. I believed you were a good man. But you involved my son in your dangerous past. A good man wouldn't do that."

"No ma'am, that's true."

Ma looked at the gun at Ike's waist. "It looks like the past has reached out and pulled you back." She stood and looked Ike directly in the eye. "My son will have nothing more to do with you." She turned toward the stove, her back to him, dismissing him.

Scared as I'd been by the gunfighter, I was more scared at losing Ike's friendship. "But Ma..." I said, starting to protest.

"Johnny, I will not have you killed in some other man's fight."

12

Ike had the look of a man kicked by a mule. He shifted his feet. "That's just it, ma'am. Johnny's in this fight whether we want him in it or not. The man I just chased out of town will be back. All he wants is to hurt me some way. He knows now the boy means something to me. He'll try to hurt him."

My ma gasped and leaned against the stove like her legs wouldn't hold her. When she turned her eyes were cold and hard.

"Then you'll just have to leave town and go far away." Her voice was harsh.

Ike looked more and more miserable. "It won't make no difference. He'll come back here first, hurt the boy, maybe even you. Then he'll go find me wherever I am."

"Who is this man? What did you do to him to make him hate you so?"

Ike looked down at his feet. "It's a long story would take a long time telling."

My ma's face was hard, her jaw set. "Ike Sanders, you will fix this thing. You will make it right."

"That is my intention, ma'am."

"You need to send for a lawman to arrest him."

"Ma'am, in the eyes of the law he hasn't done anything wrong. No lawman will come."

I'd never seen Ma lose her composure before, but she did now. "Dammit, Ike, are you telling me there's no way to protect my son from this killer?"

Ike shook his head. "We will have to protect ourselves. You have to trust me. I know this man. He'll wait until he feels the time is right. He'll look to catch us off guard."

"Is it your plan to guard my son twenty-four hours a day?"

"No, ma'am. It is my plan to teach you to protect yourselves. Do you own any firearms?"

My ma stared at Ike like she couldn't believe he was a real person.

"We have my dad's pistol and rifle," I said.

Ma glared at me, then at Ike. "You brought this down on us and now you're telling us we have to defend ourselves with guns?"

"You have to be ready in case I'm not here is all I'm saying. You have to be in the right mindset to kill this man. If you don't, he'll kill you."

"He's a professional killer! How can we hope to fight a man like that?"

"You will shoot him on sight. He won't be expecting that."

My mother was beyond upset. "You want me to shoot a man in cold blood without any warning?"

Ike clenched his jaw. "That sounds awful, ma'am, but it's about the size of it."

"And Johnny? You want Johnny to shoot a man without warning? Johnny's only fifteen. You want him to start out his life this way?"

Ike gave Ma a funny look. "I shot my first man when I was eleven. I had no choice. You don't always get the chance to be fair in life."

I watched my mother seem to cave in from somewhere inside herself. "What world have you brought us to, Ike Sanders?"

"A bad one, ma'am. But right now, it's the real one."

CHAPTER THREE

Ma held out for two days before allowing Ike to teach me how to shoot. The cowboy whose gun Ike returned to him rode by the shop the next day to tell us the Kid had returned to the trail drive. The man said he figured the Kid would finish the drive and collect his wages before coming back. The drive was headed to Abilene, so we had time yet.

The cowboy allowed as how the Kid didn't seem upset. Maybe he wouldn't come back at all.

After the man rode away, Ike shook his head. "He'll come back," he said.

It was business as usual at the newspaper. The big news around Deep Water was our own story but Ike wouldn't write it. He did allow Bill Spence to write an editorial on it but refused to answer any of his questions. Bill wrote a fancy piece with Ike as a hero who drove a would-be child killer out of town. He even suggested at the end of the piece Ike be put up for town sheriff.

Next day's news was about a calf Mrs. Winkle rescued from a barb wire fence.

Once Ma gave her consent, Ike began to teach me how to handle the Colt Navy revolver my dad left behind. When my dad died, Ma had put his guns and his other personal belongings in a trunk and locked it. I never saw her open it again until now.

The pistol was an 1851 Colt Navy. You loaded it by pouring twenty grains of gunpowder in the chamber with a little measure, stick in some wadding, then drop in the ball. Next you pulled back the lever to pack it in tight. The revolver had six chambers but Ike only ever allowed me to load five so the hammer would rest on an empty chamber for reasons of safety.

"If you need more than five bullets, I expect you're in a lot of trouble anyway," he said.

You fired the gun by pulling back the hammer which turned the cylinder and lined up the next chamber. Then you pulled the trigger.

We had a schedule we kept during those weeks waiting to see if the Kid would return. Every morning we worked at the newspaper as usual, except Ike would disappear from time to time to discreetly check on Ma. Every afternoon we'd go down into the gulley behind my house and practice with the pistol. At night, me and Ma kept the Henry rifle handy.

Ike offered to teach Ma to shoot, but she refused. "My husband taught me all I need to know about shooting a rifle," she said. Her way with Ike was cold. She'd not forgiven him one bit. I could tell it bothered him, but he never let Ma see it.

Ike made me learn everything I could about the Colt before he let me shoot it. I practiced cocking, pointing, and firing empty chambers over and over.

"The Colt Navy is a pointer gun," he told me. "Point like you would with your finger after you've cocked it and pull the trigger smoothly."

I wanted to practice drawing the pistol out of the holster, but he told me no, practice shooting it.

"It doesn't matter how fast you pull the gun if you can't hit what you aim at," he said.

I didn't think pointing and shooting an empty gun was doing much good, but I didn't argue. At first the action of thumb cocking felt awkward and caused the barrel to jerk offline but after many tries, I got better at it and could do it with one smooth motion. I was fifteen but tall for my age and my arms and fingers were long, which helped.

One day we were in the gully having a rest from practicing. The sun was high, and heat swarmed around us off the sides of the arroyo. We were under skimpy shade from a lone pinyon pine drinking lemonade my ma fixed for us.

Ike squatted there, picking up little pebbles and dropping them. "Winning a gunfight isn't about who is fast, it's about who is smartest," he said.

"Is the Kid smart?" I asked.

Ike thought about it. "He's smart enough. He knows most folks he will go up against don't have their minds made up to kill. It makes them hesitate just the slightest bit. The Kid's mind is made up before things even get started. If he's going to fight you, he's going to kill you. Simple."

Ike looked at me. "You and your ma, you both got to have that same mind set. When the Kid shows up, he's gonna fight. You shoot first and you shoot best. Don't worry about whether he pulls a gun or whether it's fair. Dead is dead. If you're alive, you can sort things out later. Dead, it don't matter."

I was about to ask him how he came to know the Kid so well but almost as if he read my mind he walked back down into the arroyo. "We best get back to it," he said.

That night I awoke from a sound sleep to the sound of a shot. I scrambled out of bed and rushed into the hallway where we kept the rifle. It was gone. I ran on bare feet into the kitchen where I found Ma kneeling at the open window with the rifle. Smoke curled from the barrel.

"Ma, what is it?"

"I saw someone skulking around out there," she said.

"Did you hit him?"

"I don't think so, but he left in a hurry."

Neither of us slept much more that night. I could hear Ma's restless turning in her bed in the next room. The next day I told Ike about it. He didn't seem very surprised or concerned.

"Maybe a deer or an antelope," he said. "It's good your ma is wary."

17

The next time I saw Ike's horse saddled I noticed the back of the saddle had a gouge in it about the size of a rifle bullet. It looked fresh. I guessed then what Ma had been shooting at that night. I figured she was a pretty good shot and that Ike would likely not be checking on us at night near as much.

About that same time Ike reckoned I was ready to try live firing. He set up a wood shingle marked with a red dot in the middle and put it on the opposite bank of the arroyo. Then he took the Colt Navy and loaded five chambers.

"You can load for yourself next time. Too much or too little gun powder can make a big difference." He handed the gun to me.

"I want you to do exactly what you've been doing, exactly the same way." Then he crossed his arms and waited.

My first shot startled me. There was a slight kickback when the gun fired, not so much as I would have thought but enough for the bullet to go high.

"Now that you know what to expect, be ready," Ike said.

This time I was, and I heard the sound of the bullet hit the shake.

"Again."

I fired again. Another hit.

I emptied the remaining chambers and every time was a hit. We walked out to look at the target. There were four holes in the upper right corner of the shingle. I felt pretty good about it.

Ike replaced the shake the way it had been. "You see how you have a tendency to aim high and to the right. Might be your eye or might be the gun. You need to adjust mentally."

"He'd have been dead, though," I said, a little cocky.

Ike didn't say anything to that. When we were back across the arroyo he suddenly spun and drew his pistol and fired five shots, all in one easy fast motion. He reloaded his Colt Army with cartridges and put the gun back in his holster, the barrel still smoking. He looked hard at me.

"He'd have been wounded. You'd have been dead," he said.

We walked back across the arroyo to the target. The shake had but one hole in it, right through the red dot. Ike picked up the shingle and dug into the dirt behind it. He came out with five bullets packed one against the next. "You've still got some work to do," he said.

I felt my pride evaporate. "Is the Kid as good as you?"

"Better." Ike watched my face. "I told you before, you got to be able to hit what you're aiming at. That's important. There's only one thing more important. That's your mindset. We'll work on that once you can place every bullet in the red dot."

I wanted to ask how he learned to shoot, how he knew the Kid so well, but there was a cold look in his eye that told me he wasn't going to talk about it. We went back to work.

There was a shadow hanging over us in those days. Ma's jaw was always tense. Ike was like a different person to me now, not just the ordinary newspaper man who set type and wrote stories. He still did that, but now I saw another side to him. He was always alert, he wore his gun even working in the shop, the Kid's rifle and the shotgun were never far from his reach.

I gotta admit it was exciting for me even with the chance I might end up dead. I guess when you're young it doesn't feel like it can really happen to you. I enjoyed learning to shoot. I enjoyed being with Ike, seeing a part of him no one else knew about. I was proud of my skill with a gun. I knew I was good.

When I was in the shop I couldn't help glancing at the Kid's gun. It lay on the floor by the wall in its holster where Ike had dumped it the day he took it from me. He never touched it after that. I had a feeling Ike didn't want me bothering it, but I studied it from the corner of my eye.

The holster was cut lower in front. I figured that was for a quicker draw. The pistol was a Colt .45 Peacemaker, you could tell that much. The wood of the grip was darkened by sweat. That told me the Kid practiced a lot. The other thing I knew about the Peacemaker was you didn't have to load the chambers the way you did with the Navy Colt. You used little cartridges all set to go that you popped into the chambers. Then you just pulled the trigger.

I wanted that gun. The way I saw things it was useless just lying there. It loaded faster and fired faster. I figured it would give me a better chance. One day I asked Ike about it.

Ike stopped what he was doing and stared at me and shook his head. That was it. He didn't say why. But that didn't stop me thinking about it.

It had been near a month since the day the Kid had come to town. One morning when I came to work, I saw a strange horse at the hitching post outside the newspaper office. It looked trail worn and dusty. Inside was the cowboy whose gun Ike had returned. The man looked at me when I came in, nodded to Ike, and left.

Ike watched him go.

"The Kid's on his way," he said.

CHAPTER FOUR

Ike sent me home to tell Ma the news. She was at the sink, washing the breakfast dishes. She didn't look surprised or alarmed. I guess you live with something long enough, no matter how bad, it becomes almost normal after a while.

I told her about the Kid's gun and how Ike wouldn't let me use it. It didn't make any sense to me and I guess I was kind of mad about it.

Ma took Ike's side. "I don't like you using a gun at all, Johnny. But we got no choice. This situation was thrust upon us and we have to deal with it best we can. We have to learn how to defend ourselves against the likes of a gunfighter. But that doesn't mean you have to become a gunfighter like him. Your father defended his home and family with that rifle over there and the Navy Colt until he died. Most of the time he didn't need either, just the strength of his character. He was a good man and people respected that, even the bad ones." Ma wiped a dish, stacked it, gave the towel a snap and sent me her firm look. "Your father's pistol is good enough for you. You don't need to use some gunfighter's gun. It won't make you better in any way I know."

I could see there was no point arguing with her. I changed the subject.

"Did pa ever have to fight a man?"

Ma got that far away look in her eyes and fetched out a chair to sit. She wiped away a wisp of hair stuck to the sweat on her forehead.

"When your pa and I met, he was a Texas Ranger. He'd been fighting Comanche and tracking outlaws for three years pretty much single handed before he was twenty. Then he went off to fight in the Civil War, but he told me he'd come back and he did. We'd lost everything we had and were poor as church mice, so we decided to move up north here to Deep Water and make a new start in a new town. Your pa never told me anything about the war. He didn't want to talk about it. But he told me about his Ranger days. He was proud that with all his arrests he only ever killed four men; one white man and three Indians. That was the kind of strength your pa had."

My ma had a way of bringing pa right into the room with her words, she admired and loved him that much. I didn't ask Ike about the Kid's gun after that.

Ike changed our lessons soon after hearing the Kid was on his way. He began to talk at me while I practiced shooting, told me stories about times when men got killed, times they got careless or lost focus. I knew what he was doing, he wanted to stiffen me up to be ready to shoot and not to hesitate.

By then I was putting my bullet in the red dot regularly from the draw. My pa's old holster was smooth worn leather and the old Navy came out like silk. I had a new appreciation for pa's outfit now I knew his story. After a day of shooting practice, we'd dig all the bullets out of the dirt. I took them home with me and at night after supper when the coals were still hot, I'd melt the lead and pour it off into the mold that had been with the pistol in the old trunk. Each day I'd have new bullets and maybe a few extra to set aside.

I started wearing the Navy Colt everywhere I went now. Its weight in the holster felt so natural that when I wasn't wearing it something seemed like it was missing. I'll admit it made me feel a bit puffed up to have it on, especially when I'd see Meghan Kline, the cute little red head, staring at it.

In that month since the Kid had left, two more trail drives stopped at Deep Water. Each time Ike went down to the Lucky 7 Saloon to talk to the cowboys. He never let me go anymore. When he came back, he'd have a story to write up. My stories were always about things happening around town, not very exciting news.

One day Bill Spence came to the newspaper office. I was surprised because he never left the saloon. I was running the printer when he spoke to Ike.

"There's two strangers at my bar asking about you," he said. "I can't say as I like the look of 'em."

Ike told him he'd come down and see for himself.

"I don't want no trouble at the bar," Mr. Spence said. "I told my shotgun guard to see to that."

After Mr. Spence left Ike finished up the piece he was writing and got up out of his chair. "You stay here, Johnny, and see to the paper. I'll be back shortly."

I stood on the boardwalk watching Ike walk down the street to the saloon. I saw the way he glanced at the two tired looking horses hitched there and the way he hesitated at the door and loosened the Colt in his holster before he walked in. Right then I decided I better go down there. I walked around behind the building and went in the back way. There was a hallway and stairs and just beyond was the door to the bar. I peered in from just out of sight.

Ike was seated at a table with two other men. He sat facing the front door, his back to me. The two strangers sat either side of him. They weren't talking loud, but the place was empty except for a card game at one of the other tables, a couple of cowboys at the bar, and the shotgun guard on his tall stool, so I could catch words now and then.

"Ain't got nothin' to do with the money now," one of the men was saying. He wore a bushy red beard with a grey streak and a flat round-brimmed hat. His trail coat was dusty, and both his hat band and coat showed sweat. "You humiliated the Kid, and he don't forget."

Ike said something I couldn't hear.

The other stranger had a black mustache and thin face that made it look larger, and he wore a dusty black derby. His eyes seemed too close together behind a beak shaped nose. His voice sounded like it came out through it. "He'll be comin' just the same."

There was more talk I couldn't hear. The thin man seemed to grow agitated at Ike's words. "We just come for our share, is all," he said.

23

Ike's reply was lost but he threw both hands in the air like he was saying he had nothing.

There was more talk with words I couldn't hear and Ike doing most of the talking, and then he pushed back his chair and stood up.

"Boys, I got to get back to work," he said.

I snuck back outside and hurried over to the shop. When Ike walked in the door, I was busy working the printer. I stopped when he came in.

"Who were they? Was there a problem?"

Ike hung up his hat and shook his head. "No problem. Just a couple of guys looking for work. They thought the paper might be hiring. I sent them out to the Flying Y Ranch to see if they had any jobs out there."

"Nobody you knew?"

"Nope."

It was the first time I knew for a fact that Ike lied to me. It wasn't a good feeling. I didn't say nothing, but it took a chunk out of my trust in him. It also got me wondering about his past life.

As I levered that print wheel monotonously up and down checking the emerging copy for smears, I thought about what I overheard in the saloon. There was no doubt from their talk those men knew the Kid. They knew he was coming and why. How did they know him?

The other thing was it meant the Kid wasn't too far away, might in fact already be here. And there was Ike at his desk going through letters and bills like nothing else existed beyond this room.

After we ate our lunch, we closed up the newspaper as usual. Ike headed to his room at the saloon and I walked home. When I got there, I was surprised to find a horse tied to the porch rail, one I'd not seen before. It was a handsome animal, well-groomed but dusty, a big stallion. There was a Winchester in a scabbard and large saddlebags stuffed full.

I thought of the two strangers in the saloon and wondered if this was one of them, but it wasn't. The man seated at the kitchen table with Ma serving him tea was a big man, muscular looking with a bony face. His eyes came to me the moment I came in the door, his look measuring but not unfriendly.

"This would be Johnny, then."

My ma nodded. "Johnny, this is Ranger Will Hanks. He knew your daddy a long time ago."

Ranger Hanks stood and reached out a long arm.

I shook it. "What brings you to these parts, Ranger Hanks?" I asked.

"Now Johnny, don't pry," Ma said.

"It's fine," Ranger Hanks said. "I'm on my way to Abilene. Came by here to pay my respects to your ma. Your pa and me were Rangers together."

"Now you set back down, Will Hanks, so you can drink your tea," Ma said.

"I thought my pa worked alone," I said.

Ranger Hanks was back in his seat and reaching for a muffin from the plate in the middle of the table. I sat down opposite him where Ma had put a glass of goat's milk for me.

"He did, mostly," the ranger said. "I did too. But every now and again when chasing Comanche, we'd ride together." He cocked an eye at me. "Your pa was a good man, a brave man." He glanced at Ma before continuing. "I mind the time he was a passenger in a stagecoach when it got held up. The shotgun guard was killed right away. A real dangerous gang. They got the Wells Fargo box from on top, but your dad stopped them from robbing the passengers. From what I heard, as soon as the stage reached the next town, your pa got on a horse and went right after the gang, all by himself. Caught up to 'em, killed one and captured two others. The leader got away, though, and the money was never found."

Ma stared at Hanks. "He never told me that story."

The ranger gave his head a slight shake, chewing on the muffin. He had light brown hair, almost blonde, and pale blue eyes. "I expect he wasn't proud of the outcome, losing the leader and the money. He was kind of hard on himself that way."

That story made me real proud of my dad. He had been a genuine hero and I never knew it.

The ranger stayed for a while, sipped tea and talked. Ma seemed pleased to have him there. He didn't say much more about Pa, but he did have a lot of questions about Deep Water. He asked me about the newspaper, how it got started and how it was to work there and all. Finally, he stretched and stood and allowed as how he should be getting on his way. I noticed he wore his pistol backward on his left side, so the grip faced out. I figured he drew his gun cross body and shot righty.

After he was gone, I grabbed some extra bullets and headed out to the ravine. Ike hadn't come yet, which was unusual for him. I wondered whether he'd had some more business with those strangers in town.

I had emptied the Colt and was loading for the next round when Ike appeared. He rode his horse up to the little tree and tied it there. Right away he began lecturing me about being more cautious.

"Did you hear my horse coming? Could you be sure it was me? If I'd been the Kid, I could've shot you before you loaded that gun."

I grinned. "I knew it was you. I know how your horse sounds."

He didn't smile. "What if the Kid had killed me and was riding my horse?"

Well, he had me there, but I couldn't see that was very likely. "I figure the Kid wants to hurt me just to hurt you," I said. "If you was already dead that wouldn't make much sense."

Ike shook his head, looking disappointed. "Point is, you can't assume anything. You got to be ready no matter what."

He was right, I knew that. But the sun was shining bright, the day was warm, and it was a long time since we'd seen the Kid. I guess I was just finding it hard to worry. Besides that, I was feeling pretty cocky about how well I could handle a gun.

Ike saw that in me and told me another one of his stories. "He was little more than a boy, a lot like you," he said, "but he was a real natural with a pistol. He couldn't miss. Folks would throw up bottles and even coins and he'd hit 'em two three times before they reached the ground. His draw was lightening quick—I never saw a faster one." Ike glanced at me. "You didn't have to ask him twice, he'd show you his draw or shoot any target you put out there, he was that proud of himself." Ike leaned back against the dirt bank, thinking about it. "He was scary good, one of those once in a lifetime talents."

I was about to shoot but I waited for Ike to finish. I had a notion how his story would end.

"One day a stranger come to town. He said he'd heard how good this boy was with a gun and wanted to see for himself. They walked out into the street together and the stranger pointed to the weathervane on a barn about a couple of hundred feet away, asked the boy if he could hit it. Quick as lightening the boy's gun was in his hand and the sound of the shot and the clang of the weathervane came at the same time. The boy grinned and turned to look at the stranger and the last thing he saw was the barrel of the man's pistol pointed at his head."

I was indignant. "That wasn't fair. That was murder."

Ike nodded, not smiling. "The stranger looked at the crowd standing around him. He told them, "You saw it. He drew his pistol and fired. I shot him in self-defense. Anybody see anything different?"

Now nobody was going to argue with a man who already had his pistol out and showed he was ready to shoot anybody who twitched. The man mounted up and rode off. Now there was a lot of people upset by this and complained it wasn't fair. But at the end of the day, the stranger rode away, and the boy was dead."

Ike shook his head in wonder. "That boy was the fastest with a gun I ever did see."

CHAPTER FIVE

By the time I walked into work next morning the entire town knew a Texas Ranger had come to Deep Water. Folks stopped me in the street to tell me what they'd heard.

"He's staying at the Box Elder Ranch," Ms. Swisher told me. "Maybe he has come to capture that gunfighter who wanted to kill you." Her old eyes crinkled behind thick glasses with happiness at the thought.

Widow McKenzie ran the Box Elder outfit. Her husband died a few years ago leaving her with a cattle ranch to run and just a foreman and one or two hands to help with it. She let travelers stay in the big empty bunkhouse in exchange for doing some chores around the place while they were there. I rode out there from time to time to follow up on a story or bring out supplies when the widow couldn't get to town.

I was surprised Ranger Hanks had stayed on since he'd told Ma he was headed to Abilene. I guessed he wasn't in a hurry to get there.

I came into the shop busting to tell Ike. It wasn't often we got a real news story to publish.

He smiled at me. "Why don't you write this one up, Johnny? After all, you already spoke to him and all."

That was the first I figured out Ike hadn't been late to meet me yesterday. He must have seen the ranger's horse tied to the porch and waited for him to leave. I didn't say anything, but I wondered why he'd shied away.

But the chance to write my own piece was exciting and I got down to it. The story Ranger Hanks told of the stagecoach robbery and my dad's part in it and how the two were Texas Rangers together made a great article, I thought.

After I'd finished, I handed it to Ike, and he read it. Then he read it again. After that, he laid it down on his desk and sat thinking. After a long spell he turned to look at me, still standing there waiting.

"It's good, Johnny. Real good. There's nothing wrong with this article at all. It's an interesting piece. But I'm wondering if we should publish it just now."

I was kind of shocked. "Why not? You said it's good. We don't get stories like this to write up very often. Besides, you told me to write it." I think I was kinda irked because it was about my pa and was personal for me.

"Yes, I did. You were excited about it and had first-hand knowledge and I wanted you to get some practice writing." He paused. "I'm not saying we shouldn't publish it. I'm saying maybe not just now."

He turned his chair to face me, leaned forward. "Ranger Hanks is a lawman, a Texas Ranger. Like it says in your story here, he has hunted down and arrested a lot of men. Killed more than a few, likely. We don't know who might pick up a copy of our newspaper and see he's here right now. Could be someone wishes him harm. That's why I think we should wait a while."

I was stunned. "But if we wait it won't be news. You taught me that."

Ike sighed. "Being a newspaperman has a responsibility. Sometimes it's important not to go to print for the common good."

"But everyone in town already knows it," I said. I never before argued about a story with Ike. I just couldn't understand his reluctance.

"Knowing something is one thing. Seeing it in print means it's true," Ike said.

I wasn't done fighting this. "How long do we have to wait? Ranger Hanks might stay a week, two weeks even. It won't be news after that."

Ike turned back to his desk. "More likely, he'll be gone tomorrow. If he's still here in a couple of days, we'll talk about it."

That was my dismissal and I knew it. I turned away and picked up a broom and started sweeping. I needed to do something to let out my frustration. I just kept getting madder. After years of not knowing I finally learned something about my pa, something heroic, and I was proud. I wanted everyone to know about it. I think it was that anger made me decide to confront Ike with his lie about the two strangers. I had not intended to say anything about it, but feelings built up inside me. I just let it out.

"You lied to me yesterday. How do I know you're not lying to me now?"

Ike was at his desk reading copy and his head jerked up. "What are you saying, boy?"

"Those two men you went to see at the Lucky 7 Saloon, they weren't strangers looking for jobs. You knew them."

Ike stood slowly and turned to face me. "What makes you say that?" His expression was cold.

I was nervous now, but I'd already put myself out there, so I had to finish. "I followed you. I went in the back door. I thought you might need back up."

"So, you overheard our conversation."

"Some."

"Sit down."

"I'm fine." I wasn't. I was nervous as a cat at a dog fight.

"Sit down." He spoke just as firm, but a little less edgy. I sat.

Ike perched on the corner of his desk. "I told you and your ma my past wasn't always pretty, that I've done things I regret. When the Kid showed up, I saw how the past wasn't going to let me go easy. Those men yesterday were part of that same past. When you live rough like I did your life is like a rock thrown in a still pool of water. Ripples keep coming. People you disturb with those ripples don't forget." Ike sighed. "Yeah, you're right. I don't want to publish your article for another reason. It's because I don't want those ripples to become waves."

I was confused. "Is it something to do with those two men?"

Ike nodded. "They are not good men and wouldn't hesitate to shoot Ranger Hanks just because he might represent a threat to them. I asked them to move on. Maybe Ranger Hanks will move on also. That would be best for everybody."

I wasn't satisfied. I knew there was more to it than that. "What about the Kid? They said they talked to him, said you humiliated him. How do they know the Kid?"

Ike shook his head like a weary man. "Johnny, when you live rough you cross paths with other men who are the same way. I think the Kid knew those men were headed this way. He wanted them to remind me he was coming, just to keep me edgy."

That was all. We both went back to work. Our lead article was about Mrs. Finster's runaway rooster. Meanwhile, the entire town was talking about Ranger Will Hanks.

That afternoon during shooting practice I was still angry. Ike had recently changed the target because it was getting too easy for me. He hung the slate off a wire suspended between two posts. Now when my bullet hit the target the red dot jumped and jerked around making the next shot much more difficult. Today in my frustration I had it jumping about like a jackrabbit.

"That's nice shooting, boy."

I jerked my head around. Ranger Hanks sat on his horse near the little tree, leaning forward in the saddle over crossed arms, watching me. I'd been so caught up in my own self I'd let someone come right up behind me, just what Ike had warned me against. There I was with an empty pistol, like a fool. I was glad it was the ranger, not someone else. I still felt a fool.

He slid down off his horse and came down the slope, watching me reload. "Who taught you to shoot like that?"

I felt uneasy about telling him the truth. I was pretty sure Ike wouldn't want me to. Mad as I was at Ike, I knew there was a lot I didn't know. "I taught myself," I said. "This here is my pa's old Navy Colt."

"I recognize it," the ranger said. "He'd be right proud of the way you can shoot it." He hunkered down. "What'd he tell you about his old Ranger days?"

I was done loading and slid the Colt into its holster. "He didn't. I was four years old when he died. Only things I know about him my ma told me."

"She gave you his gun?"

"Only recently." Here I skimped on the truth a bit. "She decided I was old enough to learn to
handle it, I suspect."

The ranger nodded. He was picking up stones in his hands and dropping them again where he squatted. He reminded me of Ike that way, like they couldn't keep their hands still.

"I imagine your ma had your dad's old gear stored away somewhere."

I nodded. "She kept some of his stuff in an old trunk. This Navy Colt, the fixings for loading, and his holster belt."

"She keep his badge, any of that stuff?" He smiled. "That'd be something to be proud of."

"I don't know what else is in there." It struck me then Hanks seemed mighty curious. I decided it was time to go down another road. "How long you staying around?" I asked.

He looked caught by surprise, then grinned. "Oh, just another day or so. Thought I could do with a rest and get the chance to know you and your ma a bit better."

The ranger stood up, stretched, and climbed back up the slope. "You keep up that practicing," he said as he mounted up. "You look near as good as your dad already." He rode off.

I walked on back to the house. Ike hadn't turned up. I wondered if he'd seen the ranger and turned around, like he did last time. Ma was heating up the iron on the stove when I walked in.

"Ike never showed up," I said. "Ranger Hanks did, though."

She looked surprised. "Well, he never came here to the house. Seems strange."

It seemed kind of strange to me, too.

Next day at the newspaper office Ike wanted to know had I heard from the ranger again.

"You never came out for pistol practice yesterday," I said.

He gave me a long look, like he knew what I was thinking. "You don't really need me for target practice anymore. What you need is considerable more work sizing up people." He shook his head. "I don't know how to help you with that."

Right about then there was the sound of a gunshot. It came from the street just outside. We ran for the door. Everyone in town was out on the boardwalk to look.

Outside the Lucky 7 Saloon a man was kneeling in the street. His flat brimmed hat lay in the dust next to him, a pistol was in his hand. He stared down at it, like he was trying to lift it and couldn't understand why it wouldn't move. His red beard glinted in the sun. As we watched, he pitched forward onto his face, then rolled over on his side and was still.

Facing him about twenty feet away was Ranger Hanks, his gun still smoking in his hand.

Next to me, Ike spoke softly.

"I think you can go ahead and print that story now, Johnny."

CHAPTER SIX

The crowd was hushed and still, just as unmoving as the man who lay in the dust before them, the man who a moment before had lived and breathed just like them. Ranger Hanks pointed the smoking pistol at two men.

"You—and you—are witnesses. I shot in self-defense." He loaded the empty chamber, then with a quick turn of his wrist holstered his gun across his body.

"Who is the law around here?" he asked.

There was a shuffling silence while people in the crowd looked at each other. Bill Spence spoke from the doorway of the saloon. "Closest law right now is you."

Ranger Hanks nodded. "Send for the district judge. I'll wait around for him." He glanced at the body. "Send for the undertaker. I'll pay." As he turned to go into the saloon his glance caught mine. His eyes showed nothing.

I turned to Ike. "Wasn't that one of your friends he..."

Ike wasn't there. I never saw him go back into the shop.

I walked in. He was scooping extra cartridges for his Colt from his desk drawer, dropping them in his pocket. He looked up at me.

"It's begun," he said, kinda under his breath.

"What's begun?"

He didn't answer me. He picked up his hat from the rack, put his trail coat under his arm.

"I got some business out of town," he said. He came to where I stood near the door. "I meant what I told you. I want you to print up that article you wrote. I want to see it in tomorrow's edition."

He gave me a pat on the shoulder and went out the door.

So much had happened in such a short time. I'd never witnessed a man die in a gunfight before, nor had I seen such cold calmness as Ranger Hanks showed during it, nor felt the strange fascination with death, like watching a coiled rattlesnake strike, that came over me seeing it.

I had a lot of questions. Had the dead man, the same man I had seen speak to Ike at the saloon just yesterday, actually tried to kill the ranger as Ike had predicted? Where was the other man with the weasel face? What did Ike mean when he said it's begun? What's begun? And why had Ike suddenly decided there was no harm in publishing my story all of a sudden? Was it the harm was already done?

I was glad Ike was letting me publish my piece. But a moment later I realized the actual news was the gunfight, not the presence of the ranger in Deep Water, not the old story of the stagecoach robbery. People would all be talking about the gunfight. The fact that my pa had ridden with Ranger Hanks would be a sidebar.

Ike had been real clear. He wanted me to print the article. But I couldn't print it the way it was. I had to include the story of the gunfight. To do that, I needed to talk to people who were there. I would have to go to the Lucky 7 Saloon.

I wasn't eager to go there, but I didn't see I had a choice. I checked that my pencil was sharp and picked up my notebook. People were gathered in front of the saloon near the body watching Mr. Phelps, who owned the general store and served as undertaker, make his preparations. I walked across the street and behind the building. The saloon's rear corridor was empty, but the bar was full. People were buzzing about what they'd just seen. Ranger Hanks was nowhere in sight.

The man I wanted was Bill Spence. He was there behind the bar helping his bartender. He saw me and came over.

"What are you doing here, Johnny? This is no place for a nice kid like you right now."

"Mr. Spence, I need to write the story of the gunfight. Can you tell me what happened?"

"Well, Johnny, I wasn't there at the start. I was in the back moving barrels. I heard loud voices and that's when I came in. By then, they was already moving out to the street." He shook his head like he was uncomfortable. "Look, Johnny, you go on back to the newspaper office. I'll send Luke, my shotgun guard, over to see you. He was there through the whole thing."

That sounded just fine to me. I turned to go but someone had a hand on my shoulder.

"Maybe it would be best to hear it from someone who was actually in the fight."

I looked around into the blue eyes of Ranger Hanks.

"Come on over to the table, Johnny, and I'll tell you all about it." He looked at Mr. Spence. "Bring us a couple of soda waters." He turned me by the elbow and steered me to a table near the wall.

To tell you the truth, I didn't know whether to feel lucky or worried. But Ranger Hanks had been a friend to Pa so I didn't expect he'd harm me. But he was a dangerous man, I knew that now. The way he'd been at the shooting, so cold and calm, was like he'd become a different person. I couldn't let go of the feeling of it.

Mr. Spence brought over two glasses of soda water and set them on the table. He didn't talk at all. He scooped up the coin Ranger Hanks put down and left.

"Drink up," the ranger told me. I took a sip. It was a hot day and heat seeped into the building like water into sand despite the fan groaning away. The drink was tingly, cool, and refreshing.

Ranger Hank's eyes held me. "I need to level with you, Johnny. I wasn't entirely truthful when I was talking to you and your ma the other day."

38

The ranger had this way of speaking made you feel you were all alone in the room. "I did have business in Abilene, but my business moved here. I was tracking a robber who'd escaped from Yuma Prison. I first heard he was in Abilene, then learned he was seen here in Deep Water. So, I stayed here."

I nodded. Thinking about the conversation I overheard between Ike and the two strangers I figured Abilene must've been where they had seen the Kid.

The ranger kept watching me as he spoke, like he was trying to read my thoughts. "Today I sat right here at this table and waited. I got lucky. The robber came in and walked up to the bar. As soon as I stood, he knew what was happening. He challenged me and walked out to the street. Almost as soon as I cleared the doorway he went for his gun. I shot him in self-defense."

"He never got off a shot?"

"No."

I was busy scribbling down his words, not watching his face as he spoke. Now I looked up.

"Was anyone with him?" I asked.

I saw a hint of surprise around his eyes. "No. Why?"

I didn't tell him what I'd seen. "I...uh, isn't it unusual for a man like that to be alone?"

He stared at me. "Not really. He's a man on the run."

"Thank you very much, Ranger Hanks." I started to stand. He put a hand on my arm, held me there half standing, his grip hard.

"These are dangerous times, Johnny. I wouldn't come in here wearing that rig anymore." He meant the Navy Colt in my holster. "Someone is liable to try to see if you know how to use it."

When he let go of my arm, I could still feel his fingers. I hurried out the back way. I glanced at Mr. Spence as I passed the bar but he didn't look up.

When I arrived back at the newspaper office, Luke the shotgun guard was waiting for me.

I thanked him for coming, had him sit near the desk, and asked him for his version of the story. At first it seemed to line up with the ranger's, then it changed.

"The ranger was sitting at the table where he sat with you just now," Luke said. "Then the red bearded man came in. He and his friend went over to the ranger's table and sat down."

"His friend?" I asked.

"Yeah, this skinny-faced man. Both of them were heeled. They'd been hanging around the place last couple of days, so I wasn't surprised to see them. Just was surprising to me they seemed to know the ranger."

"They knew him?"

"Yeah, I'd say so. They talked like they was old friends. I couldn't hear the words, you understand, just watched the way they were together."

"Then what happened?"

"Well, my attention was drawn elsewhere. We had a good crowd in the bar today. Then I heard loud talk and its coming from the ranger's table. It's not him that's talking loud, it's the other two. The ranger spoke quiet like, but they didn't like his words one bit. Then all of a sudden, the big red beard guy stands up and puts a hand on his gun. That's when I get involved. I pointed the scatter gun at them and said for them to take it out into the street. Then red beard says something like, "You wasn't planning to share at all, was you?" to the ranger. The ranger says, "Shut your mouth!" and stands up. They look like they're gonna draw on each other right there and then, so I says if they don't take it out to the street there's gonna be little bitty pieces of all of them all over the place. That gets their attention and the ranger walks on out. Then—"

"The ranger went out first?" I asked, surprised.

"Yeah. The other two talked together for a moment, then the red beard guy followed the ranger and the skinny faced guy skedaddled out the back. Seemed like from where I was the moment Red Beard hit the sidewalk the shot sounded." Luke hesitated. "Now this is just my impression, mind, but it seemed to me Red Beard was planning on talking, not shooting."

I looked up from my notes. "Are you saying the ranger never gave the red-bearded man a chance?"

Luke shook his head. "Not sayin' that. I couldn't see from my guard seat. But like I said, the shot came real soon after the man passed through the door."

Luke had to hurry back, saying he had no help today, and things were dicey at the Lucky 7.

I thought that was an understatement. But now I had a problem. I believed Luke's story. He had no reason to lie. It was clear to me now the ranger had lied. But why? He seemed not to want me to know about the skinny-faced guy. He didn't want me to know he knew both men. He wanted me to think he shot in self-defense when according to Luke's story he never gave the red-bearded man a chance.

But what could I write? The ranger had told me what he wanted me to write, but it wasn't the truth. But if I wrote the truth, I'd have a very dangerous enemy.

What about the rest of the ranger's story? Was the red-bearded man really an escaped convict, or was that a lie too? Who was the skinny-faced man?

In the end, I did exactly what Ike wanted me to do in the first place. I published my original story without changing a word.

CHAPTER SEVEN

Ike was fine with that. He never came back that day but was at his desk next morning looking over the copy I'd printed. He looked up and smiled as I walked in.

"You'll make a newspaper man yet, Johnny. This here is a good issue. Well done."

"I was worried I should write something about the shooting," I said. "After all, that's the real news. I don't even know the name of the man got killed."

"Don't you worry about that. I'll write something today."

He did write something. It wasn't much, just a simple outline of the event everybody in the street already knew. Mostly it was the ranger's story—a wanted man enters the saloon, the ranger tries to arrest him and it ends up in a shootout with the bad guy dead. A hearing is delayed pending the arrival of the circuit judge, blah, blah, blah.

I could have written that much. There was a name, though. Ike gave the man's name as Ewan O'Brien.

That afternoon when I went home the ranger's horse was tied to the porch rail. He was seated at the kitchen table again. This time, Ma sat across from him. I could see Ma liked him being there. She looked different, her face a little flushed, her hand pushing a strand of hair away from her face. I hadn't seen her look like that before and was thinking she was real pretty. Their talk was so low I couldn't hear what they were saying as I walked in.

They both looked up, a little furtive like kids caught at something they shouldn't have been doing.

Ranger Hanks gave me a smile. "Hello, Johnny. Me and your ma been catching up."

Ma jumped up. "Sit down, Johnny. Let me get you some milk."

Something inside made me uneasy. I guess after seeing the hard side to Ranger Hanks I was bothered by the attention he was paying my ma. I couldn't say that out loud, though.

'No thanks, Ma. I got some chores to do."

I walked out of the kitchen and went to my room, sat down on my bed. I tried to sort out why I was so troubled. Ranger Hanks was a dangerous man, alright. But thinking about it, he had to be that way to do his job. My pa did the same job once, so I guessed he likely had a dangerous side to him too. Maybe I was judging the ranger too harshly. Still, something about the whole gunfight incident didn't set well with me. I couldn't help my feeling about it.

I wondered if Ma had heard about the gunfight yet.

I went out the back way to the shed to check on the goats. It was little more than a lean-to, open on the goat's side so they could come in for the shade and get water. There was a door on the outside with a wooden wedge that pivoted to secure it. It was open now. Ma must have seen the ranger coming and, in her hurry, forgot to latch the door, and the wind caught it. As I reached for it, a small gust of wind blew it toward me. At the same time, I felt a hammer-like blow hit the door right near my hand and heard the sound of a rifle shot.

I just stood behind that thin door trying to figure what happened and of a sudden it came to me and I threw myself into the shed and onto the hay-strewn dirt floor. I was shocked. I'd been shooting a lot of bullets lately but this was the first one coming at me and there was something a whole lot different about that. The sound of a gun aimed toward you is not like when its pointed somewhere else. You know it right away. But I wasn't thinking about that right then. I was trying to figure out who shot at me and where from.

I heard my ma scream my name from inside the house. I guess Ranger Hanks probably kept her from running right out the door looking for me. She would've wanted to. I called out I was fine and to stay put. The ranger called out asking where the shot came from. I told him a direction but couldn't say much more than that. He called back to me to stay in the shed until he'd had a look around.

About five minutes later the ranger showed up at the shed door. He was walking with his horse, keeping it on the shooter side of himself. I was sitting on the floor cross-legged, my pistol in my hand, just waiting.

Ranger Hanks looked down at me. "You make any enemies, Johnny?"

"None I know of," I said. I didn't tell him about the Kid. I needed to talk to Ike first, although by now I was wondering who I could trust.

"Well, whoever it was, he's gone now." He stood pondering it. "Maybe he saw my horse out front and thought you were me."

I'd not thought of that but I preferred it.

He beckoned me out. "Let's go take a look."

He was still leading the horse. I got up, kept the Colt in my hand and followed him. We walked north in a straight line following the angle of the bullet as it came to the door. It took us across the main road in front of the house.

Ma came out on the porch. I called to her to get back inside, we'd let her know when it was safe.

We crossed through coyote brush following deer trails and up a slope covered in buffalo grass to the top of a knoll. Just behind it we found horse prints in the dust. The horse was shod. In one place you could see the horse had been standing a while. We followed the hoof prints behind the knoll and along an arroyo and back to the main road. We found prints coming and going. The house was out of sight where the prints came to the road.

"The shooter come out from town," the ranger said.

"Could've been anybody," I said.

44

We walked back to the shed. The bullet had passed through the door. We searched the brush beyond but never found it. I guess I didn't really expect we would.

We went back inside. Ma was making tea. Doing that seemed to help her when she got upset. We told her we didn't find anything.

I saw Ma was getting ready to ask a question, and I worried she might mention the Kid, so I shook my head at her, but the ranger spoke up and saved me the trouble.

"Louise, don't you worry. I'm going back to town now and ask around. I'll find the shooter."

Louise? I was surprised to hear Ranger Hanks use Ma's first name. They'd gotten to feeling more friendly than I knew. I didn't feel comfortable with it.

After the ranger left, Ma asked me, "Was it the Kid?"

"I don't know, Ma," I said. "I don't know if he's around, but he could be, I guess." But in my heart, I was pretty sure he was. I needed to talk to Ike.

"I'm going back to the newspaper office," I told her. "I need to finish up some work."

She shook her head. "Johnny Whittaker, there is no way I'm letting you go out now after someone has taken a shot at you."

"Ma, it's just as likely someone thought I was the ranger out there. He said so himself."

"I don't care about the ranger. I care about you."

I couldn't see what that had to do with me riding to town. "Ma, we can't just hide away like a ground squirrel in a hole. I'll look sharp and be careful and I'll come right back as soon as I finish my work."

Ike was still at his desk when I walked in the newspaper office. I glanced at the wall. The Kid's stuff was still there. I sat down in the other chair near the desk.

Ike looked up.

"Someone just tried to bushwhack me at the goat shed. If the wind hadn't caught the door, they might've got me."

Ike's eye went right away to the Winchester leaning against the wall. "I suppose the Kid could be here with new weapons." He looked back at me, studied me. "It just doesn't feel like him, what you describe. The Kid would want to be sure I knew it was him. He'd of shown himself or left some sort of sign. You didn't see anything like that, did you?"

I shook my head.

He looked closely at me. "How are you, Johnny? How's your ma? That's pretty upsetting."

That's about as tender as I'd ever heard Ike sound toward me. Or maybe it was for my ma.

"It's good Ranger Hanks was there to help with Ma." I watched his face while I said it. Surprise flashed across, then I saw worry.

"Ranger Hanks was with your ma?"

I nodded. "Second time he's been out. He talks to her about my pa. I think hearing about it does Ma good."

Ike nodded his head like he understood, but it didn't change the worried look.

I got back on the subject. "If it wasn't the Kid, who could it be?"

Ike's chair creaked as he leaned back. "Well, now you mention the ranger was out there, how do we know it wasn't someone wanting revenge for the shooting of O'Brien?"

46

"Ranger Hanks said that, too. Maybe it was the other feller who was with O'Brien looking to even the score."

"Pernelli? Could be, I guess." He didn't sound convinced.

That's the first I'd heard the other man's name. "How'd you know those men?" I asked.

Ike gave me a contemplative look. "I told you before, you live rough, you meet rough people along the way."

That was the end of it as far as Ike was concerned.

After that day, Ranger Hanks started coming out to the house regular. He was almost always there when I came home to practice shooting. I didn't like him paying attention to my ma that way, but I tried not to show it because I saw it meant a lot to her. She went to extra trouble to look nice and dress up more than usual and she just seemed to have a glow about her. I didn't want to spoil it for her after all those years of unhappiness since pa died. But it still bothered me.

Ma started getting after me to stop my pistol practice. She thought it wasn't necessary any more. "It's been months since that awful man left," she said. "And now that Ranger Hanks is here he won't dare to show up. Why don't you just set and talk with us when you come home?"

I told her I didn't think that's what the ranger wanted, and she showed some color and looked away when I said it.

Truth was, I wasn't near as confident as she was the Kid wouldn't return, even with the ranger hanging around. I never forgot those black cold eyes and the deadly moves. I didn't figure he'd be put off by much of anything. He said he'd be back and I believed him.

Ike took to being away more those days. He had me take on more responsibility with the newspaper. I was writing more of the stories, formatting the publications, even choosing the editorials. The paper had grown since the gunfight. There was a new tension in the town, it seemed like. People wanted to know what was happening. Our issues were a full two pages now, front and back, with a solid advertising section.

Ike never told me where he went. He was at the office when I arrived in the morning, then he'd load up his pocket with cartridges, take his rifle and ride off. I never asked. But that changed when the circuit judge arrived.

Mr. Phelps was the one poked his head in the door that morning to tell us. "He's setting up his court in the Lucky 7 Saloon," he said. "Court's at two o'clock this afternoon." He scurried along to spread the news.

Ike was at his desk when Phelps came, just putting shells in his pocket. He put them back in the drawer after that and settled back at his desk. He glanced at me. "Johnny, I'll handle reporting on the court proceedings. I need you to watch over the shop."

I nodded. I didn't say anything, but I was real disappointed. After all, it was me running the paper day to day while Ike was off somewhere. I found the stories, wrote them up, set the type, ran the proof. All Ike ever did was glance over the proof and tell me go ahead. Only once or twice did he find anything wrong. So, I felt I deserved a chance to report a big story like this one, probably the biggest story ever to happen in Deep Water.

Yeah, I was miffed.

When I came back from my lunch and pistol practice it was about half past one. When Ike saw me, he put away what he was working on, picked up his notebook. I noticed he was wearing his gun belt.

"I didn't think the judge let people into the courtroom wearing guns," I said.

"Mebbe, mebbe not," Ike said. "But I plan to be armed getting there and getting back." He grinned at me. As he did, I realized he hadn't done that so much lately—grinning, I mean. He used to grin all the time.

He came over and put a hand on my shoulder. "When I get back, I'll need you to help me finish the story."

After he'd gone, I thought about that. It was a real complement, asking me to finish his story. It was like saying I could write it better than him.

There wasn't much to do hanging around the shop with the real story happening at the Lucky 7 Saloon and everyone who might otherwise drop by to pass along some gossip crowded into the saloon instead. I figured I was probably the only one in town not at the court hearing. Turned out I was wrong.

I was sweeping the floor for maybe the fifth time that day when a shadow came across it.

CHAPTER EIGHT

The man was in the doorway with the sun directly behind him, his features hidden in shadow. But I could tell enough to see he was pointing a gun right at me. He stepped just inside and away from the door and I saw who it was right then. The weasel faced man, Pernelli. Those too-close-together eyes had a nasty look to them. So did the pistol pointing at me.

"Drop that gun belt," he said.

I was wearing the Navy Colt. Since I wore it all the time, I'd pretty much forgotten about it. When he told me to drop it, I was sort of surprised. Some gunfighter.

I was mad at myself for letting him get the drop on me so easily. But there was nothing to do but obey, so I uncinched the belt and let it slide to the floor.

He waved his gun barrel for me to step aside. He kept waving it until I was standing by the wall. Then he stepped forward, picked up the Navy Colt and stuck it in his belt. After that, he went over to the wall where the Kid's weapons were stacked. He holstered his own gun and picked up the gun belt. He slung the rifle over his arm and kept it pointed in my direction.

He didn't say anything. He didn't have to. He walked back to the door with his arms full of guns and disappeared.

I wanted to chase after him but what could I do without a weapon? We'd just gone from a room full of guns to none at all. All I could of done was throw a letter opener at him. This day was not going well.

I heard his horse shuffle its feet outside and the sound of it trotting off. I went to the door, peered around carefully and watched the back of him leaving town. At least I knew what direction he was headed. Then I saw he'd left the Navy Colt on the boardwalk. The day got a lot better then. I felt ashamed at letting Pernelli get the drop on me but I'd have felt a whole lot worse if I'd lost my pa's gun.

I had a thought of picking up the Navy Colt and chasing after him but let it go. This was over for now and I'd made enough mistakes already. I holstered the gun and went back inside and thought about what it all meant.

Pernelli wasn't stealing the Kid's guns. You didn't steal the Kid's guns and stay healthy. That meant just one thing. He was retrieving them for the Kid. That meant the Kid was close by. Real close.

A sudden panicky thought came to me. With Ike and the ranger and everyone else in town packed into the Lucky 7 Saloon, Ma was at the house all alone with no one to protect her.

Lucky thing I rode our horse back to the office after lunch. The way Pernelli rode out of town was opposite the way to our house. There still might be enough time. I jumped on the horse and headed home at a gallop. The place was quiet when I arrived. After a nervous glance up toward the knoll where the shooter had been, I tied off the horse at the porch railing and rushed inside.

Ma was not in the kitchen. She wasn't anywhere in the house. There was no note. Everything was in order, no sign of a struggle. The barn, the goat shed were both empty. No Ma.

By now I was worried sick. Ma never went anywhere. If she had to go to town, she always told me or left a note. I'll admit it, I was real upset. I sat down on the porch step and came close to bawling. I was sure the Kid had Ma.

After sitting there pretty much useless, feeling sorry for myself, I got to my feet and mounted up and rode back to town. It was time to find Ike and tell him how things stood.

There were two men with rifles acting like guards at the saloon door. The town was making a big deal out of this hearing. Ike was just inside the door perched on a stool. The judge and the ranger were over at the bar. Bill Spence was there too. Every table was filled and people had pulled up chairs and stools where they could. The judge was talking when I stepped in but I wasn't listening. I was focused on Ike.

He saw me right away, saw the look on my face and came outside with me.

"What's wrong, Johnny."

"Ma's gone," I said. It came out kinda choky.

He looked hard at my face. "She ain't at the house?"

"No."

He grinned. "Well, boy, that's because she's sitting right in there." He pointed inside at the crowded room. Sure enough, after a bit of looking there she was at a table next to Mr. Phelps. I felt the fool for sure. But a happier fool.

Ike kept staring at me. "Was that all?"

By the time I finished telling him what happened his face changed to a grim look. He grabbed me by the elbow, and we walked fast over to the newspaper office. When we got there, he pulled his rifle down off the wall and went to his desk and loaded his pocket with shells, just like he'd been doing each morning. He was talking to me the whole time.

"You did right, Johnny. You did right to go look to your ma like you did. Pernelli taking those guns can mean only one of two things."

Two things?

"It means the Kid is somewhere real close by or it means the Kid is dead. Those are the only two ways Pernelli would dare come take his guns."

Dead. The Kid might be dead! The thought had never even crossed my mind. It was a good thought.

I glanced at Ike. Loading up his pockets with shells the way he was, I figured he didn't think it was that second possibility. "You think Pernelli and the Kid might have partnered up?"

"It's possible," Ike said. "Real possible."

When we came to the door, Ike said, "Johnny, I want you to go back to the Lucky 7 Saloon. Keep your ma there until I get back. Don't leave her alone, you hear me?"

"Where are you going?"

"I'm going to track down Pernelli. Maybe I can catch him before he hooks up with the Kid."

"I should come with you," I told him. "The ranger will look out for Ma."

Ike gave me a funny look. "You're the one cares most about your ma. Remember that. You stay with her no matter what." Then he went and mounted up and rode off the way Pernelli had gone.

After he'd gone, I walked back to the Lucky 7 Saloon. I brought my reporter notebook and a pencil. I figured I might as well get the story if Ike wasn't there.

I took the stool Ike had left. My ma glanced around and saw me and smiled. I smiled back.

The judge was talking. "You all heard the ranger's story. You heard those two witnesses corroborate it. Anyone here got anything else to say?"

The room was quiet.

Mr. Spence spoke up. "My shotgun guard was here the whole time. He can tell what he saw."

I noticed Mr. Spence didn't look at the ranger while he spoke.

"Where's this shotgun guard?" the judge asked.

"Right here, your honor." Luke's hand went up.

53

The judge picked up the bible, handed it to the man next to him. "Take this and pass it to that man."

When the bible got to Luke, the judge had him give his name and swear to tell the whole truth.

I could tell Luke wasn't happy about this but his boss had put him on the spot, so he told it like he told it to me. When he was done, the judge looked over at the ranger. "Seems to be some inconsistencies between your stories."

The judge was a florid faced man with a large head that wobbled on thick shoulders. His bushy eyebrows met in the middle giving a stern look when he raised them. He was raising them now.

"I guess he thought he saw what he saw," the ranger said.

"Did two men come and sit at your table, one of them being the man you later shot?" the judge asked.

"When I looked up, I saw one man standing there," the ranger said, his tone mild. "If he came in with someone else, I don't know. He may have stepped toward my table, but he didn't sit down."

The judge looked at the shotgun guard. "Where is your guard seat, sir?"

Luke pointed out the high chair. "Right there, your honor."

The judge looked back at Ranger Hanks. "What table were you at, Mr. Hanks?"

The ranger pointed at the other side of the room.

The judge nodded, seemed to reflect. He studied the ranger. "Are you sure about who left through that door first?"

"Best of my recollection it was the deceased, your honor."

The judge shifted his gaze to Luke. "You saw nothing that went on outside the building, that correct?"

54

"Yes, your honor."

"Anyone else see anything?" the judge asked.

There was another long silence.

"I find Ranger Will Hanks shot in self-defense," the judge declared. He smacked his gavel down on the bar. "This hearing is adjourned."

A minute later, as an afterthought, he said, "The bar is open."

Most folks pushed their way to the bar then. The ranger shook a few nearby hands and came over to Ma. He smiled and listened to what she was saying but his eyes darted around the room as if looking for someone. When they lit on me, I went over.

The ranger looked at my notebook and pencil. "Got your story, son?"

I nodded. "I got a couple of them," I couldn't help saying.

His eyes narrowed, then he laughed. "It's something a Texas Ranger has to deal with every day," he said. "There's always more than one story, depending on how you want things to turn out." He smiled down at ma. "I sure do appreciate you coming here to support me."

Ma smiled and colored up a tad.

"I need to leave you with Johnny for now," Ranger Hanks said. He touched his hat brim and walked over to talk to the judge, who was part way done drinking a glass of beer over at the bar.

"I looked for you at home," I told Ma. "I didn't expect you'd leave like that and no note."

She put her hand on my arm. "Oh, I'm sorry, Johnny. I was flustered, I guess. I decided last minute to come here to support Will. I just wasn't thinking good." She smiled. "We can go home now, if you like."

I remembered what Ike told me about staying in the saloon. But I didn't know why and I couldn't think of a good reason to keep Ma there, so I told her okay.

It was near noon. The street was mostly empty. If people weren't in the saloon, they were inside shops and houses out of the hot sun. We walked toward our horse hitched to the rail outside the saloon.

"Leave the lady and step out into the street." It was the Kid's voice.

My innards scrunched up at the sound. I whipped my head around and there he was. He wasn't there a second ago. Now he was in the middle of the street, standing easy, legs square, waiting like he'd been there all day. The high sun was slightly behind him and gave him kind of a halo.

He looked the same as that time in the bar, the same black felt hat with the leather vest. He wore a white shirt like a gambler wears, the sun making it shimmer at the outline of it. I couldn't see his eyes but I could feel them, like black holes. His black pants and black boots all blended together making one shadow, like a wraith had floated out of some grave and into the street.

I felt the same sick fear I felt all those months ago. All my cocky bravado I'd built up with my shooting practice wasn't there anymore. I was hoping not to pee myself.

He waited, saying nothing just like the last time.

It was my ma made the first move. She was at the hitching rail when he spoke, I was near it and the horse beyond us. I had turned, my eyes on the Kid. Now I felt Ma move back toward me like she was going to the sidewalk out of the way. I felt mighty lonely right then.

Next I knew, I felt a tug at my belt and Ma was next to me and the Navy Colt was in her hand. I heard the click as she cocked back the hammer and a shot sounded. Dust kicked up in the road just at the Kid's feet.

He didn't move an inch.

I couldn't turn my face away from him, those invisible black eyes held me like I was in a dream. I heard the Navy Colt cock again and another shot and another spurt of dust near the Kid's legs and he still didn't move.

By now people were pouring out of the saloon, brought by the gunshots.

The Kid whistled. I heard galloping hooves and out of the alley alongside the saloon came a great black stallion, saddled, short reins trailing, sliding to a stop on extended hooves right in front of the Kid, blocking him from our view with his body and the rising dust, and then the Kid was up in the saddle and horse and rider disappeared back into the alley and were gone.

And I swear, just before it disappeared the stallion looked directly at me with its right eye, just as black and empty as the eyes of its master.

CHAPTER NINE

The Kid was gone. I took the pistol from my ma's shaking hand and holstered it. I was feeling pretty shaky myself.

Ranger Hanks came pushing through the crowd. He stood looking down at the two of us from the edge of the boardwalk.

"Who was that?" he asked.

"I never saw him before," Ma said, "but he wanted to kill my son."

The ranger looked at me. His voice was terse. "I told you if you wear that rig someone will try you. You could have got your ma killed."

I didn't bother to respond. I saw some of the folks who had come out early enough to see what happened looked at Ma with new respect. Not many of them would have dared do what she did, I thought.

"Let's go home," I said, and took Ma's arm.

The ranger stared at me. "You watch out for her, son. I'd come along but the judge has a few more questions for me." He turned and walked back into the saloon.

I figured the judge should have a few more questions for him, but I doubted he'd ask them.

Ma rode the horse and I walked alongside her on the dusty road home. I tried to talk gentle to Ma about Ranger Hanks. "Ma—"

She cut me off short. "Johnny, I know I was wrong in what I did back there but I couldn't stand the thought of something happening to you and I just got so angry with that...that...creature I couldn't stand it. I wanted him dead."

I stopped right there and looked up at her. I'd have hugged her if she were walking with me. "Ma, it's over. With anyone else, at any other time, you'd maybe have got us killed. But this time you saved us. I ain't angry with you."

"Why didn't he go ahead and shoot?" Ma asked.

"I wish I knew the answer to that. My guess is it all has to do with Ike. This man wants to goad Ike into a fight."

"Where was Ike? I thought I saw him at the hearing."

I told Ma what happened with Pernelli, the narrow-faced man. And how after that I came looking for Ike. "When I told Ike what happened, he loaded up his weapons, told me to keep you there in the saloon and then left."

"Why did he want that?" she asked.

"I figure to prevent exactly what happened with the Kid."

"I *knew* that was the...the Kid." Ma could barely bring herself to say his name.

We were nearly home. I took my chance. "Ma, you ought to know I interviewed Luke, the shotgun guard, just after Ranger Hanks shot that man. He told it to me then just like he told it today at the hearing."

Ma's chin stiffened. "I think the judge realized how far away Dusty was, that he could be mistaken despite what he believed." She glanced at me. "Besides, the important thing happened out in the street where Luke couldn't see. There were two witnesses who saw the other man draw first."

Her chin was set and she was staring straight ahead. I decided this talk had best wait for another time.

We weren't home ten minutes when we heard the galloping of hooves along the road. Ma was just pouring tea. I grabbed the rifle and went and stood on the porch. I saw it was Ike. His horse was all lathered up.

He slid off at the porch and flipped the reins up to me to wrap.

"Your ma at home?"

I nodded.

"She okay? I can see you are."

"Come on in," I said.

Ma saw Ike and her chin set tight all over again. "I just don't know what to make of you, Ike Sanders. If my son didn't set such store by you, I'd send you packing. Set down, now you're here. Johnny, fetch another cup and saucer."

Ike stood for a moment by the chair. He was dusty and sweaty from his hard ride. He stared at Ma's back for a moment, sighed, and sat down.

"Mrs. Whittaker, if what I heard is correct, I don't know whether to think you are exceptionally brave or incredibly stupid, no offense intended."

She turned to look at him with the tea pot in her hand and gave a slight grin. "Mr. Sanders, here am I thinking you are exceptionally brave or incredibly stupid to say such things to a woman with boiling water in her hand."

Ike grinned at that and put both hands up in surrender.

Ma poured his tea. Ike did look a little nervous during the pouring. He looked at me. "Tell me about it."

I did. When I finished, including the ranger's last statement, he shook his head slowly.

"I never should have left," he said. "I figured Pernelli would be headed to the Box Elder Ranch. It's a good place to stay out of the way and he left town in that direction. I figured to catch him returning the guns to the Kid." Ike scratched his head. "I guess the Kid outsmarted me." He looked at me. "Did the Kid have his own gun?"

60

I hung my head. "I couldn't tell. He never drew his gun. I didn't see things real clear."

Ike put a hand on my arm. "He's real scary to face up to." He glanced at Ma. "That makes what your ma did real brave."

Ma looked at me with a smile. "If you had children, Ike Sanders, you'd understand. But I don't understand why he didn't kill us. My shots weren't even close."

"I think it was the strangeness of it," Ike said. "When a solitary man like the Kid goes in to a fight, he's got it all worked out in his mind. He knows the man he plans to kill. He's studied him. He knows the words or action he'll use to make the man go for his gun. That way, he knows what you'll do before you know yourself." Ike looked at me. "That first time he faced you in the saloon, he studied you. Maybe he'd of shot you if you picked up the gun. It would have been easy enough. But that wasn't his plan. He wanted you to compel me to come face him. You did, but it didn't go the way he intended."

Ike looked at Ma. "You see, Mrs. Whittaker, when he faced the two of you in the street, he expected you to move away. His plan was set on how to kill Johnny. But when you moved toward Johnny and took his gun, the Kid had no plan for that. He had no plan for a gunfight with a woman. So, he did what he had to do. He ran."

Ma shuddered. "He must be furious at me."

Ike shook his head. "No, ma'am, the Kid isn't angry. He isn't even thinking about you. He don't have feelings like that, they'd only get in the way. He'll just make a new plan."

It all began to make sense to me. It didn't make me less fearful, though. After my second encounter with the Kid all my bravado built up over the weeks was gone.

"Did you find Pernelli?" I asked.

'He was at the Box Elder Ranch, like I guessed. But he didn't have the Kid's guns and he denied ever having them."

I looked at Ike in disbelief. "How can he say that? He came right in and took 'em at gunpoint."

"I wouldn't get overly concerned about it," Ike said. "He'll say pretty near whatever he needs to make the problem go away."

Ma was looking at Ike. "You know this man?"

"I did know this man, once upon a time. But we went different ways."

"Why is he here?"

Ike sighed, glanced at me. "Like I told Johnny, here, a man lives a rough life and meets rough men. When you try to take another road, the past seems to always want to tag along. Pernelli and O'Brien came here because of me. We rode together for a time and they kinda looked at me for leadership. Then they did some things and went to prison. When they got out, five years later, they drifted some then came looking for me." He shrugged. "Lookin' for more leadership, I suppose."

Ma was staring intently at Ike. "You said "when they got out". You mean when they escaped."

Ike shook his head. "They didn't escape, ma'am. That's a fact you can confirm over the telegraph wire to Yuma. They served their time."

Ma just kept staring, her jaw set.

I spoke it out loud. "The ranger either lied or was misinformed when he said O'Brien was an escaped convict."

Ike glanced at Ma, sighed again. "Ranger Hanks knew O'Brien and Pernelli were in prison. He might not have known they were out legally."

I wasn't going to let it lie. "The ranger said he was tracking an escaped robber he heard was in Abilene, then here. He made it sound like it was official business. But it couldn't have been official, could it?"

Ike didn't say anything.

"If it wasn't official, why was he tracking him?" I asked.

Before Ike could answer my question, Ma interrupted. "You said the Ranger Hanks knew they were in prison. How do you know that?"

Ike swung his head to look at Ma. "Because he put them there."

CHAPTER TEN

My head was buzzing with all this new information and I could tell Ma was wrestling with the same thoughts. She was mad as a hornet thinking Ike kept all this from us. She stood up, walked to the sink and stood with her back to us.

I was pretty mad too. I tried to follow the rope to its end.

"So, if you knew O'Brien and Pernelli and they looked to you for leadership and Ranger Hanks put them in prison, you must have known Ranger Hanks."

"I knew of him, for sure."

"And the Kid knows Pernelli enough to send him for his guns. The Kid came here looking to kill you. What's the Kid's tie-in to all this?"

Ma had turned back around and was watching Ike's face now.

Ike sighed for about the fifteenth time. "The Kid's father rode with us sometimes. There was a shooting. The Kid's father got killed. I believe the Kid blames me for it." Ike looked at each of us. "He's wrong. I had nothing to do with his father's death but he won't believe that. He'll just keep right on coming."

Ma said, "It seems to me what I said before is true. If you go away the problem goes with you. I won't have my boy die just so this angry young man can have his vengeance on you. You should leave right now and go far away. It's the decent thing to do."

Ike shook his head. "I wish it was that easy. I really do. But it isn't." He stood, picked up his hat. "Everything I've told you here is true. But its more complicated now. I got no family of my own. The Kid knows that. I have special feelings for you folks. The Kid knows that too. That's why it doesn't matter whether I go away or stay. He'll still try to harm you, just like he thinks I harmed his pa."

He looked back at me from the door. "Johnny, I'll be at the newspaper office if you need me."

Ma and I listened to the hoof beats die away.

Ma came and sat down at the table. She reached out, put her hand over mine. "Maybe we should just leave, Johnny. What Ike says may be true, but I find it hard to believe this Kid would follow us very far. He would want Ike to know what he'd done if he hurt us but if we are a hundred miles from here, Ike couldn't know. I think this is our only choice."

She was right, and I knew it. It was the best of a lot of bad choices. But it made me angry and maybe more stubborn.

"Ma, we can't just run away from everything you, me and pa built here. We would have nothing. We can't sell the property without alerting the Kid. Where would we go? What would we do?"

Ma looked tired and defeated. "We'll find a way, Johnny. I know we will."

I hated that she'd been brought to this through no fault of her own by complete strangers.

"Ma, I'm going to go talk to Ike. He got us into this and he needs to get us out. You keep the rifle close. I'll be back soon."

Ma didn't answer me, she just sat there staring blankly. That's the way she was when I went out the door.

Back in town, the streets were empty but there were a lot of horses tied up at the Lucky 7 Saloon and you could hear the sound of many voices. It was like the whole town was in there celebrating with Ranger Hanks.

But I didn't think he deserved being celebrated. If you put Luke's story together with Ike's, it came out that Ranger Hanks didn't give O'Brien a chance. The ranger told those two witnesses what to say, so you couldn't go by their testimony.

I was confused, going back and forth about who to believe. I'd begun to trust Ranger Hanks who sure seemed to want to look out for Ma for pa's sake. Now, though, I was swinging back to thinking

Ike was the man to trust, even though he'd gotten us into this mess from the start.

As I tied up at the newspaper office, I had in mind to put pressure on Ike to get this thing resolved.

But Ike wasn't there. His rifle was gone. I checked his desk drawer and saw his extra shells were gone too. Well, I wasn't going to wait around for him this time. I figured he'd gone out to the Box Elder Ranch, maybe to get more information out of Pernelli. I decided to follow him.

I knew the Box Elder Ranch pretty well. If Ike went out there to see Pernelli, he likely went to the bunkhouse where the guests stayed, rather than bother the widow at the big ranch house. The road to the Box Elder followed the creek, mostly dry. It was shaded by cottonwood trees. This was the main road led on up to Indian Territory to the north and after that to Abilene. The Box Elder turnoff was about three miles out. There was a gate with an overhead sign and a pair of ruts headed east through the tall grass up a long slope and over a rise. I reached down and unlatched the gate.

The ground around the gate showed it was well traveled lately. Shod horse tracks were stamped over one another, some looked fresh. I couldn't single out Ike's horse in particular.

I followed the entrance road about a mile but where it sloped down toward the grove of trees surrounding the ranch, I stayed on high ground just out of sight behind the crest of the ridge and rode east a bit until I was opposite the bunkhouse. My thought was to watch the place from there, out of sight, and see what happens.

There was no sign of Ike, his horse wasn't at the hitching post but there was a corral just out of sight among the trees. His horse might be there along with Pernelli's mount, maybe tied to the railing. I dismounted, held onto the reins and squatted behind some Coyote brush. I figured to give it a few minutes.

It was pleasant there, half shaded by the brush, the sun warm where it speckled through, the tangy sweet smell of rosemary somewhere nearby. I might have begun to doze; my eyes had closed when a rifle's sharp retort sounded and rolled around off the hills and buildings. My startled horse jerked the reins in my hand, and I gripped tight instinctively, but my eyes were focused on the bunkhouse where a figure was crumpling toward the ground.

It looked like he'd come from the bunkhouse, maybe headed to the outhouse. His coat looked just like the barn coat Ike wore, the one with the pocket he stuffed with cartridges, but the figure was too far away to tell. I crouched, staying under cover of the brush trying to peer out to find the shooter but couldn't tell where the shot had come from.

The man on the ground didn't move. Where he was, the shot could have come from anywhere except the east side of the bunkhouse. It could have come from the ridge I was on or even from the ranch house.

I wanted to ride down the slope and see who it was lying there, but I didn't dare. If someone had shot Ike, maybe I'd be next. My heart was flapping like a flight of quail. The shooter might know I was here and even now be aiming his rifle at me. I could duck down out of sight, but I couldn't hide my horse which at the moment was jerking on the reins and shuffling nervously.

Seconds crawled by like men walking to the gallows. I figured all I could do was run. I formed a kind of a plan in my brain to leap onto the mare and gallop back the way I'd come but then I heard the sound of hooves. Someone was doing what I was thinking. The shooter, likely. The sound was somewhere to the west of me along the ridge and fading.

I waited. Ten, maybe fifteen minutes passed. The sun had shifted from the shade and rose higher and hotter. I was baking, sweat was in my armpits and trickling down my back. The man lying down below never moved. When I dared to stand, my knees felt creaky and tight and pain shot through the stiff muscle. I waited there a moment like a man facing a firing squad wondering if standing up was a mistake.

When nothing happened, I made myself walk slow down the slope leading the mare. As I picked my way among yucca and sage, part of me wondered when I'd feel the punch of a rifle bullet. The other, more curious part wondered who the man was lying there in the barn coat.

About a hundred feet out I knew it wasn't Ike. The coat was similar in color but not at all like his. The man's hat had fallen away and I saw black hair and thought for a moment it might be the Kid but then I saw the head was too narrow and I knew who it was. Standing over him I looked down at the too-close-together eyes and the thin black mustache. There was a hole in his temple and his head and shoulders lay in a pool of blood beginning to jell in the sun. Pernelli wasn't going to run any more errands for the Kid.

My eye caught motion and I saw someone was coming from the ranch house at a fast walk. I saw the sway of skirts and knew it must be Widow McKenzie. She was holding a rifle. I waited there for her. When she got close, she saw who I was.

"Johnny Whittaker, what are you doing here?"

"I didn't do this."

"I don't expect you did. I don't see you holding no rifle." She came close and peered down at the dead man. "I knew he'd be trouble. I don't generally turn away anyone looking to board who pays up front but I almost changed my mind just from the look of this one."

I didn't say anything.

She looked down at the body for a while then looked at me. "You didn't answer my question. What are you doing here?"

That was a hard question to answer. I didn't want to admit I was here looking for Ike when he maybe didn't even come this way. But I had no other excuse for being there. I just couldn't think of a single reason.

But the widow spoke quick before I could say anything. "Were you here scouting up a story to write?" She studied me, holding the rifle across her body with both arms. "I like you, boy. But I don't

68

generally like reporters because they always poke their noses into other folks' business. They always stir up a hornet's nest."

Widow McKenzie was tall and big boned with a broad sun darkened face and high cheek bones. Her hair was graying with the blonde hair of younger years still showing through and she wore it flung back and held there with a single braid. Her blue-green eyes studied me.

"Do you know this man?"

Another difficult question. "I think I saw him in town once or twice."

Her eyes narrowed. "What kind of story were you scouting up?"

I thought about that. I didn't want to just make up something silly, like checking on her chickens. She'd likely catch me in a lie anyway, so I went with the truth. Part of it, anyway.

"I heard you had a boarder and wondered who it was."

She looked at me shrewdly. "You wondered if it might be the gunfighter who threatened you in the saloon?"

So, everybody knew about that. I hung my head. "Yeah, I guess."

She came close, put a motherly arm around my shoulders. "Johnny, you should know I'd never allow the likes of that man to stay at my ranch. Rest easy with that thought." She looked down at Pernelli. "Well, I guess we better get someone out from town to see about burying this man. Should have a lawman look at him too, I suppose." She looked at me. "You going back to town?"

I nodded.

"You could probably get that Ranger to come out here," she said. "Best get someone."

I agreed. Widow McKenzie wanted to give me some buttermilk before I left but I felt like we needed to tell Ranger Hanks right

69

quick. Besides that, I was curious to know where Ike was all this time. I mounted up and headed back.

As I rode, I turned things over in my mind. There were lots of people could have shot Pernelli. Even some stranger. But there were three I knew who might have a reason. Ike sure could've done it. The ranger could've done it, like he did Pernelli's friend. And the Kid could've done it, maybe to keep him quiet. Did the killer know I was there? If it was the Kid, he could have shot me right then. But maybe he figured I might become a suspect and liked that idea better. And why did Ranger Hanks shoot O'Brien? Did his reason apply to Pernelli too?

I wasn't so sure Hanks was a back shooter or ambusher. He was not the one tried to kill me at our goat shed. That left Ike or the Kid, but Ike wouldn't try to kill me. He had no reason. That left the Kid, or Pernelli.

Fact was, Pernelli was dead, but I was no better off than I was when I woke up this morning.

CHAPTER ELEVEN

Ranger Hanks wasn't around when I entered the Lucky 7 Saloon. Two cowboys sat at a table playing cards and drinking whisky and looking like they could scarcely keep their eyes open. Mr. Phelps was at the bar having his supper and talking to Mr. Spence. I came up to the bar and Mr. Spence sidled over my way.

"I'm looking for the ranger," I said.

"I expect he's up in his room," Mr. Spence said. "He already had his dinner. Want me to call him?"

I nodded. Mr. Spence went into the back to find the barman and have him get Hanks. When he returned he asked me if I'd like something. I shook my head.

Mr. Phelps stood and started groping in his pocket for money for his meal.

"I'd appreciate it if you didn't leave just yet," I told him. "The ranger may need you."

He gave me a look that wasn't happy and sat back down on the stool. "Better bring me a whisky," he said to Mr. Spence.

Right about then Will Hanks walked in. He came and stood by me. "Hello, Johnny. What can I do for you? It's gettin' kind of late, isn't it?"

The man had a way of making me feel six years old, like I was up after my bedtime. It annoyed me. "Sir, there's a dead man out at the Box Elder Ranch."

"You don't say." Hanks sat on the stool next to me. "Do you know who it is?"

"Yes, sir. His name is Pernelli."

"Rocco Pernelli, eh?" the ranger said.

That's the first I'd ever heard Pernelli's first name. But Hanks knew it.

"How'd he die?" Hanks asked.

"Someone shot him with a rifle when he came out of the bunkhouse to use the outhouse."

I heard Mr. Phelps mumble under his breath. "A man can't even take a pee."

The ranger wasn't listening to Phelps. He was studying me. "Where were you at the time?"

"I was just arriving at the ranch. I was up on the ridge above it." I had this feeling I needed to be careful just how much I told.

"Why were you going there?"

"I was looking for a story. When we haven't got anything for the newspaper, Mrs. McKenzie generally has some kind of news I can write."

The ranger's eyes were boring into me. "That it?"

I shrugged. "That's all there is."

"Did you see it happen?"

"I heard the shot and then found him dead when I got there."

"Where was he hit?"

I put my pointed finger at my temple. "Right through there."

The ranger glanced around at Spence. "I suppose I'd better be getting out there. It's near on dark."

He looked at Mr. Phelps. "Guess I'll be needing you too."

"He'll still be there in the morning," Mr. Phelps said, hopefully.

Will Hanks shook his head. "Can't count on that. Better bring the wagon." He looked at me. "Can you come back with me and show me?"

"I got to see to Ma," I told him. "Widow McKenzie is there, she can show you."

Ranger Hanks headed back to his room to get his slicker and long gun.

My gnawing stomach told me it was dinner time, but I wanted to stop by the newspaper to see if Ike was there. I'd just done a whole lot to protect him and wondered if I'd been wasting my time.

He was there at his desk writing something. He looked up when I came in. "What are you doing here, Johnny? You should be home with your ma. It's pretty near dark."

Ike's rifle was in its usual place, I noticed.

"Where were you today, Ike?" I asked. "I came back here after we talked to Ma but you were gone."

"I had some errands to run on the way here."

"Did you go out to the Box Elder Ranch?"

He cocked his head, looked at me kinda strange. "No. Why?"

"Someone shot Pernelli with a rifle from hiding this afternoon. Just like someone shot at me."

"Was Pernelli hit?" Ike was standing now.

"Pernelli is dead," I said.

Ike kind of slumped back into his chair again. He dropped his head. When he picked it up, he had a determined look on his face. "Things are happening real fast now, Johnny." He looked down at his desk. "The circuit judge leaves tomorrow crack of dawn, headed for Fort Worth. I spoke to him. He promised to take a letter I wrote asking the territorial judge to send out the U.S. Marshal. I'm just finishing it up."

"But we got a Texas Ranger," I said.

"We got a ranger, but he's a little too close to the problem." Ike signed his name on his paper and folded it, put it in an envelope. He lay down the envelope and applied hot wax to the closure. "When the judge gets to Fort Worth, he's gonna check on whether O'Brien was an escaped convict or a free man. Won't make any difference in the verdict, he says, but will help the U.S. Marshal who comes out to know what he's dealing with."

I was surprised and a whole lot annoyed. I'd been asking that very question with no one paying attention to me. Better late than never, I suppose, but I felt kinda bitter about it.

"Meaning Ranger Hanks could've known all along O'Brien was a free man," I said.

"Might have, might not have."

"What difference would it make?"

"It takes away his reason for prodding O'Brien into going for his gun. If Hanks wanted to make an official arrest, that's one thing. That was what Hanks told the hearing. But if he simply wanted the man dead and pushed him into a gunfight, that's a different matter."

"Luke, the shotgun guard, told me he didn't think O'Brien wanted a fight."

Ike nodded. "I don't think so either." He stood up, loaded his coat pocket with shells.

"Where are you going now?" I asked.

"I'm going to take this here letter over to the circuit judge. Tonight, I'm going to sleep across his doorway to keep him safe. Tomorrow I'm gonna ride with him all the way to Fort Worth to make sure he gets there with the letter. Then once I know a U.S. Marshal is coming, I'll head back."

Ike sure took me by surprise. He was taking this real serious. I wondered why Ranger Hanks lying about O'Brien being an escaped convict concerned Ike so much he wanted a U.S. Marshal to come to Deep Water.

Ike took me by the arm. "Johnny, you got to look out for your ma real good. The Kid's around somewhere and Ranger Hanks ain't quite what he seems. I'm gonna close the newspaper for a few days while I'm gone. You should stay home with your ma, keep a lookout."

"What do I do if Ranger Hanks rides out to talk with Ma, like he does?" I was getting kinda anxious about this whole situation.

"You just act like normal. You don't know where I went." Ike grinned. "Most times you don't anyway, right?" He was at the door, flipped the "closed" sign around.

"But what about the Kid?"

"Chances are good the Kid will follow me. I'm kinda expecting it. Might be best, in the end."

Ike grinned, stepped out onto the boardwalk. I followed him, waited while he locked the door. It was nigh onto evening, two or three stars were out, the gas lights were on in the Lucky 7 Saloon glaring yellow through the windows like bright flowers. The street was empty. A dog barked somewhere, as if to test the silence. You could smell meat cooking somewhere.

We just kind of stood there for a few minutes, saying nothing. Then Ike spoke softly, almost gentle. "Johnny, there's a mite more going on around here than you know about. It involves Ranger Hanks and the Kid and one or two others who might come along later that you ain't even seen yet. It goes way back, but it's all comin' to a head here and now." He started to step away.

"It involves you, too," I said, not letting him off the hook.

75

He stopped, pondered me. "I think you always knew that," he said. His face had the look of a man wrestling with something deep inside him.

"Johnny, there is something else you can do while I'm away, if your ma will let you." He stepped closer, spoke softer. "Look through that old chest of your pa's, the one where your ma kept his guns. Look at everything in it."

"What am I looking for?" I was puzzled. What did my pa's things have to do with anything?

"Look for anything unusual, anything you didn't expect. There might even be something in there your ma doesn't know about."

I was feeling annoyed now. It felt like Ike was trying to find me something to do to keep me busy like you would a child to keep his mind off things.

He looked close at me seeing my annoyance. "You see, Johnny, all that's going on, well...it involves your pa, too."

CHAPTER TWELVE

It involves your pa, too!

Ike's last remark rang in my mind, echoed and re-echoed. I was baffled and growing more annoyed by the minute. Here was Ike wanting to lay the blame for the danger he brought to my family back onto my family itself.

"How can you even say that!"

Ike shrugged, turned away. He walked to his horse, tightened the cinch, and swung aboard. He looked down at me. "Maybe now's not the time," he said.

As he rode off, I stood planted there on the boardwalk like a tree, held motionless by my righteous anger. How could the man even think of saying my pa was involved in anything he and his outlaw friends might have done in their past? How could he even imply they had anything in common? Hadn't Ranger Hanks told the story of how pa single handed rode out after the stage robbers after defending the passengers?

Yet doubt crept in.

I stood there another five minutes before walking over to the Lucky 7 Saloon to retrieve my horse. The thought ate at me all the way home. One thing for sure, I was not going to burden my ma with what Ike said.

Ma had been holding our dinner on the stove and looked a bit worried when I walked in. I apologized, told her about the shooting of Pernelli and me reporting it to Ranger Hanks. I made the shooting sound like I was miles away so she wouldn't imagine I was in any danger. Still, it was a scary story to tell and I could see Ma was frightened by all these shootings.

"Who does Ranger Hanks think done the shooting?" she asked me.

"He didn't say."

She was watching my face. "Where was Mr. Sanders?"

"He was working at his desk when I went to the office."

"What did he say about it?"

"He was real upset. Right after that, he told me he was sending for the U.S. Marshal. He'd written a letter and was sending it with the circuit judge to Fort Worth. After I told him about Pernelli, he decided to ride with the circuit judge to make sure he got there safe."

Ma was setting the food on the table. "Well, maybe that's good, although I think Ranger Hanks can handle things. But it wouldn't hurt to have more law around here, way things are going."

I sat down at my plate.

Ma stood there a minute holding the pitcher of goat's milk, looking at me. "But what about this gunfighter? Won't he go ahead and try to hurt us while Mr. Sanders is gone?"

"Ike expects the Kid will follow him instead. I guess he figures he'll make an easier target for the Kid riding along on his horse."

Ma sat down. She fiddled with her spoon, not eating. "I'd have guessed that monster would more likely try to hurt us while Mr. Sanders is gone off to Fort Worth so when he comes back, he'll see what's been done."

Somehow what Ma said seemed more likely to me, too.

I told Ma Ike had closed down the newspaper for the time he was gone. We agreed I'd stay at the house. We looked at ways to get the chores done without exposing ourselves to rifle fire. We'd keep the window curtains closed and the rifle handy.

Ma didn't want me to go to the arroyo to practice my shooting, but I told her I needed to stay sharp, and besides, I'd have the Navy Colt right there and ready and she could cover me with the rifle from the house. It would be mighty hard for the Kid to sneak up on the arroyo with someone watching from the house. She finally agreed but she wasn't happy about it.

It was hard, though. It felt like prison to me, just knowing I couldn't go off wherever I wanted to go. Never mind I probably wouldn't have gone off somewhere anyhow, it still felt frustrating.

When one of us needed to go to the barn or the goat shed the other covered with the rifle. We'd always take the shortest route, never at the same time of day, always a little hesitant or jerky so no rifleman could get a real bead on us.

It was no way to live. After the first day we were both nervous as cats, ill-tempered, and dead tired.

My mind kept going back to Ike's last remarks, sayin' pa had somehow been part of something long ago that was the cause of all the goings-on here in Deep River. His challenge to me to look through pa's things kept going around in my head. I knew I'd have to do it to have any peace of mind.

I brought it up at the end of that first day while Ma and me were at the table, our dinner plates in front of us, untouched. "Ma, I'd like to see pa's old things."

She just looked at me tired like and half smiled. "I figured you would, sooner or later. But why now? We're both pretty tired and we've got to be on watch tonight."

"Doesn't have to be now. Maybe in the morning when the light is better and we're both a little fresher."

She reached out her hand and laid it over mine. "We can do it together. I haven't been through things in that chest for a long, long time. Might feel good to do it now."

The next morning after breakfast and chores Ma and I went to her room. I'd been in there a thousand times growing up but this time I noticed things, like how much of pa's stuff Ma had kept. His serape was slung over the chair back, his boots nearby like he was coming any moment to pull them on. The chest was against the west wall.

I'd always thought about it more as a bench because Ma kept a couple of cushions on it.

The day was promising to be hot, the sun was bright, and a clear blue Texas sky wrapped around everything. Ma's bedroom was cool. We were both tired from our night watch but I was excited to see my pa's things. I sat cross legged on the floor while Ma pulled items out one by one. There was a lot of clothing, some of it mine, tiny shirts and such I wore as a baby. Pa's shirts were clean and pressed and neatly folded.

"I reckon some of these might fit you now," Ma said.

There was a cloth sack. Ma reached in and pulled out a string tie, some mother of pearl buttons, a couple of sleeve garters, and a badge. The badge was a simple five-point star made from a Mexican five-peso coin. Ma told me pa never had a badge when he did his rangering, but she had wanted him to have one and had it made after they was married.

There were some documents tied up with ribbon—land title, marriage certificate, and such important papers. There was another bundle of letters, correspondence between Ma and Pa when he was fighting in the war. Ma looked sad when she pulled them out.

The last thing in the trunk was something large tied up in an old piece of leather. Ma undid the ties and laid it out on the floor. It was a bowie knife with a straight metal hand guard. The wide blade sparkled like new, but you could see from the wear on the handle that it had been used. There was no sheath with it which I guess is why it was wrapped in the leather. I picked up the heavy knife and held it in my hand, felt the balance and the sharpness of the blade. The knife was like a small sword. There was something fascinating about it. I wondered if pa had killed any men with it or maybe a bear.

Ma had picked up the letter packet and you could see she was reliving some of their times together. I put the knife down and was starting to wrap it back up when I noticed some kind of writing on the lighter side of the leather scrap. I took it over by the window and looked closer at it. Stuff was scratched on it. There were dots in a straight line connecting little squares, some tiny parallel squiggly lines and a group of upside-down vees like maybe they was meant to be mountains. I figured it was a map.

I showed it to Ma.

She took it, held it this way and that, tried to make sense of it. She shook her head and handed it back to me. "I've never seen this before. I have no idea."

"Well, it sure can't be near here. The nearest peaks are hundreds of miles away."

Ma nodded. "No, I don't believe it was made around here. Your pa wrapped up that bowie knife after he returned from the war. He did it like it was a symbolic end to the past that he wanted to put away forever."

I studied the map again. "Whatever this means, it's from long ago and likely something he never returned to, or why keep it?"

"Unless just to wrap up the knife," Ma said.

Ma was practical like that but I didn't think pa carried that leather scrap while fighting in the war just to wrap a dirty knife. I had a feeling whatever the map led to was still there.

Then I got to wondering if this scrap was what Ike had meant me to find. It surely was the only thing in the chest that might have any interest for people beyond me and Ma. But what? The thing was, the map didn't tell what it led to. I had an idea Ike might know.

But if Ike knew what the map was for, that meant he had known my pa or at least knew about him. Why hadn't he let on about that? That made two people in Deep Water who knew pa, Ike and Ranger Will Hanks. I told Ma my suspicions.

Ma didn't think that old leather scrap meant anything but she agreed not to let on to anyone that we'd found it. If Ike asked, we'd say we didn't find anything we didn't expect to find in that old chest. If he asked any questions more specific, we'd know he knew about the map.

All the answers lay with Ike, I reckoned, and he wouldn't be back for several days. Meanwhile I was chafing at the notion of being a prisoner in my own home but there wasn't anything I could do about that. Ma and I had to look out for one another.

Just about then a goat coughed. Goats are strange animals to those who don't know them and even to us that do. They can sound almost human sometimes. Once when a goat got caught in the fence, she called out with a sound just like a drawn-out cry of "help". But when a goat sounds an alarm, it coughs.

Ma went for the rifle. I went to my room where the Navy Colt was holstered and hung over my chair. I peeked at the goats first. The ones I could see were facing south, away from the road. I went to the south window in Ma's room and nudged the curtain aside just a speck with the colt's barrel.

There was the boom of a rifle and the window shattered. I dropped to the floor. There was a thud in the wall right where I'd been standing and at the same time another boom sounded. Then came two rapid fire rifle sounds from nearby. Ma was firing back, must be from the south facing kitchen window. I poked the Colt barrel out where the glass had been and fired twice in the general direction where the booming had sounded.

There was no return fire. Everything was quiet.

"Are you okay, Johnny?" Ma called out.

I told her I was fine. There was blood on my hand where the glass had cut it but that was nothing. I looked up at the wall where the second rifle shot had struck. The wall was solid here in Ma's room, with thick outer planking and an interior wall of pine and mud-daubed straw in between. Pa had built a solid, warm house. But there was a hole right through where I had been standing. The only rifle I knew could do that was a Sharps. That accounted for the booming sound. I hollered to Ma to stay low to the floor. Then we waited.

But that was the end of it. Maybe someone just wanted to see if we were paying attention.

CHAPTER THIRTEEN

Ma was a mess. She was the bravest, smartest lady I'd ever known but the danger and worry had wore her down to a frazzle and when I went into the kitchen to find her, she was huddled under the window with a white-knuckled hold on the rifle and tears streaming down her cheeks.

She looked at me as I came in and said, "I just don't know if I can do this anymore."

I didn't say anything, just sat on the floor next to her and wrapped my arms around her and hugged her like she was a baby. No words, just comfort.

After a while I said, "We'll manage this somehow, just like we always done before." I held her a little longer until I felt her stir and then we both stood, a little awkward like. Ma didn't like to show herself weak in front of me and I felt a little funny babying her.

"That last rifle bullet went right through the wall," I said. "The only rifle I know can do that is a Sharps." I thought about it. "I don't know anybody owns a Sharps here in Deep Water."

Ma glanced out the window, then went and sat in a kitchen chair. "If he can shoot us through the walls now, I guess there isn't much we can do." Her voice had a weariness to it.

I confessed to Ma. "Ike told me before he left there might be one or two other strangers coming along who are part of this thing. Maybe one of 'em brought along the Sharps."

Ma looked defeated. "I don't know what we can do," she said again. "We're trapped here. If we try to ride away, they'll shoot us. If we stay, they can shoot us right through the wall."

I didn't have an answer for her. It seemed that way to me, too.

Then there was the sound of hoofs coming quick toward the house. I took the rifle from Ma and went to the window. A man was riding hard toward the house. I rested the rifle on the sill of the open window and took careful aim. I came near to pulling the trigger when Ma put her hand on my arm.

"Wait," she said. "It's Ranger Hanks." She ran to the door.

I kept the rifle on him anyway as he jumped off his horse and tied up quick and came to the door. Ma let him in. I thought she was going to hug him at first but she didn't.

He saw me with the rifle. "You thinking to shoot me, boy?" he asked, a thin smile on his face.

Ma said, "Will, thank God you are here. Someone's been shooting at us."

Hanks looked solemn like at Ma. "Now that I'm here they won't shoot anymore."

Ma said in a burst of breath, "Thank God."

I said, "Why not?"

Ranger Hanks studied me for a moment. "Smart boy, just like your pa." He turned to Ma. "They won't shoot just so long as they get what they want."

Ma stepped back. Her hands flew to her face. "You are with them," she breathed. I could see the realization crushing her.

Hanks' face gave nothing away. "No. But I need what they want."

"What is that?" I asked.

"The map."

I didn't look at Ma when I spoke. "What map?" I still didn't look at Ma, hoping she would play along.

Hanks looked from one to the other of us. "The men out there believe your husband made a map of where he put the Wells Fargo money box after he chased down the robbers."

"But he never found the money," Ma said. "You told me that yourself. Sage never told me that robbery story, he never told me about any map. They are mistaken."

Ranger Hanks sat down in a kitchen chair without so much as an invite. He kept looking at Ma with a steady gaze, like he was going to pull out of her what he wanted to hear.

"Those men have waited a long time and ridden a long way to find you. The war got in the way and some of the boys ended up in prison for a spell. Your husband did a fine job of hiding away up here after the war. No one knew where to look for you for a long time. Now they found you and they aren't going to believe you don't know anything about the map."

"How did they find us?" I asked.

Hanks looked at me. "I think you know, boy."

I thought I did too. I thought about Ike and how he came here and after a while started up the newspaper and hired me. That paper with his name on it, real or fake, would have found its way around and later there would be my name as assistant editor. Whittaker.

Hanks could see I figured it out. He went to the door and whistled. We all sat at the kitchen table and waited. Then there came a knock at the door and a man came inside. It was Ike Sanders.

I could only stare. He'd lied to me. He hadn't gone with the circuit judge to Fort Worth. No U.S. Marshal would be coming to Deep Water.

"Hi, kid," Ike said.

I didn't look at him, I didn't say anything. Ma tightened up like she does when she's real upset but she didn't say anything either.

Ike kept talking. "There's a couple of things I left out of what I told you, Johnny."

Ranger Hanks grinned at him. "I don't suppose you told him you were the leader of the outlaw gang, did you, Ike?"

Right then the door was pushed open and two men I'd never seen came in. One of them had the dark skin and black hair of an Indian and carried a Sharps rifle. They stood at the kitchen entrance and waited. Both wore gun belts and looked like they'd been sleeping rough.

Ike said to me, "Johnny, did you look through your father's chest like I asked?"

I didn't look at him. I just nodded.

"Did you find anything?"

I shook my head.

One of the men, the skinny one, said, "We can make this as tough as you want, kid." He stared at me with mean little eyes.

Ike waved a hand at him to shush. "We don't need none of that."

Ma stared at the man. "There is nothing in my husband Sage's chest that would interest you except maybe a clean shirt which you could certainly use."

"We're gonna have to see for ourselves, ma'am," the man said.

Ike looked at Ma. "We're going to take a look around the place. Once these men find what they're looking for they'll go." He nodded toward the two men who were already moving into the other rooms.

Ranger Hanks stayed at the table. "They are going to search the house," he said. "They're not the most refined of men so things could get messy. It would be best to just give them what they want." Already we heard banging coming from the bedrooms.

I spoke quick before Ma could answer. "We can't give them what we don't have," I said. Ma was strong but I didn't know how much of this she could take. Here these men were tearing up her home, our lives, right under our noses and we couldn't do a thing. Ma was a private person and this intrusion must be tearing her up.

Ma was staring at Ranger Hanks with a look of disgust. "How long have you been a part of this...this gang? Back when you were riding with my husband?"

Hanks gave a little embarrassed smile. At least he had the decency for that.

"I'm not a part of the gang. Never was." He glanced at Ma, quickly looked away. "When Sage Whittaker went after that gang and broke it up, I heard the leader had escaped and the money was gone. I didn't learn anything different until after the war when a member of the gang was up for parole at Yuma Prison. I was sitting on the parole board at the time and the prisoner told me he could show me where the money was hidden in exchange for my vote. I agreed." He shrugged. "It was a lot of money. Once he was out, though, the story changed. It turned out he knew who had the money, but not where it was."

Hanks paused, glanced across the room where Ike was just leaning against the wall, waiting and listening. Hanks went on.

"The man told me Ranger Sage Whittaker had found their camp, shot him in the arm, captured him. He'd caught their leader, Ike Sanders, too. Ike already hid the money away somewhere, but they didn't know where. While the man was tied up, he'd seen Ike and your husband whispering together. That night Ike somehow managed to escape. Your husband didn't even try to catch him. The man figured they'd struck a deal. He always figured Ranger Sage Whittaker knew where the money was. Then during the two days it took for Sage to bring him in, the man noticed Sage looking at a map."

Ike kept his gaze on Ranger Hanks but didn't say anything.

Hanks grinned at him. "The newspaper idea was real clever. Sanders rode under a different last name as an outlaw, but he was always Ike." Hanks laughed. "There's a lot of Ikes in this world but once you put that together with the name Whittaker, you got something to ponder. I happened on a copy of the Deep Water Liberty News and saw Ike Sanders, Editor, and Johnny Whittaker, Assistant Editor. That combination of names made me curious so me and Ewan and Rocco rode out here together to see what we could learn."

"Ewan O'Brien," I said. "The man you shot and killed."

Hanks sighed. "Once I got out here and got a good look at the Editor-in-Chief over there, I knew he was the leader of the gang and I'd have to fight him or join him. I figured it was better to join him on account of he'd gotten close to Sage's wife and son and maybe had information I needed. Then I got to looking around and realized how many ways we'd have to split up the money. I couldn't see how I needed Ewan anymore, so..." He shrugged.

"I guess you didn't need Rocco anymore, either," I said.

"I guess not."

Ike still said nothing.

The crashing and banging sounds had stopped. After a while the two searchers came back in the kitchen.

"Well?" Hanks asked.

The man with the Sharps shook his head.

The other man, skinny as a hat tree with dark wells under his eyes said, "We tore it all apart. There's nothing there."

Hanks' words came harsh. "Search this room and then go look in the shed and the barn. It's here someplace."

"I'll search the shed," said the skinny man and went out the door. The Sharps man they called Cherokee Bill began pulling everything down from the kitchen shelves. Flour soon coated the floor like a snowstorm and sugar and molasses added to the wintry mix.

Hanks looked at Ma while this was going on and said, "You could have saved yourself all this."

Ma didn't look at him or answer.

After he'd emptied or broken everything possible Cherokee Bill turned to Hanks and shook his head. It was then I saw something that made my eyes grow wide. My father's bowie knife was tucked in his belt, wrapped in the leather map like it was a sheath. I glanced at Ma. I could tell she'd seen it too.

CHAPTER FOURTEEN

It was another hour before the two gang members returned from the shed and barn. We'd been hearing a lot of protest from the goats while the men tore things up out there. They came into the kitchen and shook their heads and showed empty palms.

Ma said, "Why can't you believe we don't have a map. Sage never said anything about one."

"I think you've got everything you can get from us," I said. "We got nothing more to give you."

"Maybe they buried it," the skinny man said.

Ranger Hanks turned to Ma. "Where is it, Ellen?"

He spaced his words and put a nasty edge to them. I saw Ma tense up. There was a table knife not far from my hand. I knew I'd be shot before I could reach it, but it was the only move I had. I'd die before I'd let them touch Ma.

Ike moved away from the wall and came to the table and put both palms on it and leaned in. He looked into Ma's eyes.

"Mrs. Whittaker," he said, "I know you for a God-fearing woman. Do you swear under the eyes of God you don't have the map?"

Ma nodded. "I do swear."

Ike stood straight and looked at Ranger Hanks. "That's it, then. The map ain't here. I know this woman and her reputation. She don't lie."

Ranger Hanks stared at Ike and then Ma. He shook his head like a man shrugging off a hard punch. His chair scraped as he stood. He glared at Ike. "Where else could it be?"

Ike stood, looked back at Hanks. "Maybe he put it somewhere safe, like a bank."

"This town doesn't have a bank." You could feel the anger in Ranger Hanks' voice.

"Most people here let Bill Spence up at the Lucky 7 Saloon keep valuables for them. He's got a safe," Ike said.

They all looked at each other and started toward the door.

"Hold on." It was the mean-eyed skinny man. "What about these two?"

"What about them?" Ike asked.

"We can't just leave them here. They'll raise the alarm."

"By the time we ride in and start blowing up Spence's safe the alarm will be raised anyway," Ike said. "You can take their horse if that'll ease your mind."

The man muttered his way out the door.

Ma and I sat still like statues and listened to whistles as the men gathered their horses, the sounds of mounting, and hoof beats pounding off into the distance. We didn't hear anyone go to the barn for our horse. I guess they figured it wasn't worth the trouble.

I got to admit I was trembling sitting there, kind of a reaction sort of thing but frightened and angry too. Ma looked as white as I ever saw her. I was mad, but I didn't know who to be maddest at, Ike or Ranger Hanks. I kept trying to think who we could turn to but there wasn't anybody.

Ma said, "We've got to warn Bill Spence."

"How, Ma? By the time we get the mare saddled they'll be halfway to town. We got to look out for ourselves. When they don't find pa's map in Spence's safe, they'll come back here."

"Where can we go?" Ma asked. "If we try to run, they'll catch us for sure. We only have the one mare."

I had an idea. "Ma, we can go to the Box Elder Ranch. I spoke to Widow McKenzie and I know she'd help us. She could give us another horse, if nothing else. And that gang won't think to look there for us."

Ma thought about it and agreed.

We took the rifle and shells and some clothing and money we had around and loaded it up on the mare. We left feed for the goats and filled the water trough to the brim. Then we set out taking the back way around town to Box Elder Ranch. It was a tense journey, slow from my need to walk and lead the mare, full of imaginings of a killer bursting from the brush or a single shot from the Sharps rifle ending one of our lives.

It was late afternoon when we approached the ranch gate. At the ranch house, Widow McKenzie saw us coming and came out on the porch to greet us. She was drying her hands on the apron she wore over her long dress. Her dog sat on the porch eyeing us intently with one ear up and one ear down.

When she saw who it was, the Widow came rushing down the steps. "Why, Ellen Whittaker, welcome. What brings you here?"

Ma slid wearily off the horse. "Susan, I am so sorry for this intrusion. I'm afraid we bring nothing but trouble, but we had nowhere else to turn."

"Oh, bosh," the Widow said. "You come on inside. Johnny, bring your things along. Tom will care for your horse." The hired man was approaching from the barn as she spoke.

The Widow took Ma by the elbow up the porch stairs. I unpacked the bundle of clothing and took the rifle along. Tom took the mare to the barn to unsaddle her and give her a rubdown. I felt as safe and comfortable now as I had felt in a long time.

Widow McKenzie led Ma to the kitchen and sat her down at the table and gestured for me to sit next to her. "Let me fix some tea and you can tell me about it," she said.

93

"We don't have much time," Ma said. "They could find us gone and come after us any time."

The Widow put her hands on her hips and said, "Now who might that be?"

Quick as she could, Ma told everything that had happened. The Widow bustled about the kitchen as she listened, putting water to boil and laying out cups. When Ma was done, she stood still, thinking.

"Seems to me what we need is a plan. I won't have you two running off in the dark with a gang of killers chasing you. But we do need the law involved. The proper law, that is."

She poured hot water into a tea pot and brought the pot to the table. "Let that steep for a few minutes. I got some fresh cookies I made up for the boys in the bunkhouse." She took a tray from near the stove and set it on the table. The cookies were warm and sure smelled good.

The Widow sat and began to pour. "Here's what we'll do. I got two fellas I hired on in the bunkhouse. I got Tom. I got another feller bunking in for the night. I don't know the man but he don't look like no robber. More like a drummer, I'd say." She looked at me. "How's them cookies?"

I nodded, my mouth full of cookie.

"This wouldn't be the first time we forted up here and held off bandits or Indians or what all. I'll ask Tom to saddle up and ride to find the closest law he knows of and bring it back here. We'll bring the bunkhouse boys in to enjoy these cookies and post a guard. Soon as those bad boys show up, we'll send their scalded butts right back to town."

"One of 'em has got a Sharps rifle," I said.

"That don't worry me," she said. "This old house was built to protect against attack from Indians, robbers, and Mexicans back in the day. These log walls are thick enough to stop a cannon ball. Did once, in fact. Once we pull them shutters closed on the windows, we can shoot them, but they can't see us. There's nothin' for them to hide behind for a long way out."

Ma still looked worried. "But when it's dark..."

The Widow laughed. "When it's dark, Scamp here can hear an ant crawling along and point it out. He'll keep watch." The dog came to her when he heard his name and she roughed his neck fur. The one ear still hung down.

She stood up, then. "I done enough talkin' for this month. You two stay and enjoy the tea while I get things organized." She bustled out the door with Scamp right behind her.

Widow McKenzie had a way of making you feel safe, like she had everything under control. It felt good to me right then and I could see Ma relaxing a bit. But questions about pa nagged me.

"Could it be true, Ma? Would Pa really keep the money and hide it, like they said?"

Ma shook her head. She was firm. "Your father was as honest and forthright as anybody can be. He'd never hide away money for himself, money that belonged to someone else."

We both sat quiet for a bit. I could see she was thinking about it.

 "You know," she said, "the war got started right quick after that robbery happened. Your pa was on the trail of those bandits a long time. If your pa had recovered the chest and done something with it, he didn't have much time before the war started up and he went off to fight. We'd just met, fallen in love, and we were going to marry as soon as he came back. That he came back was miracle enough. We had no money, no belongings and didn't care. Your pa borrowed the money we needed to build here in Deep Water and paid it off with income from the goats and hired out work once in a while. If he had such a treasure hidden away, there never was a better time to go find it." She looked at me. "He never mentioned it."

"But the map..."

She shook her head. "It could mean something else entirely, or nothing at all."

The porch door creaked, and men came into the kitchen, herded along by the upbeat banter of Widow McKenzie. The men carried rifles. We heard the sound of receding hoof beats and knew that Tom was on his way. But who knew how long it might be until the law descended on Deep Water?

While daylight held out one of us took a turn at watch, peering out each window for any sign of movement. We didn't know when they would come or if they'd come at all. One thing sure, they couldn't stay in Deep Water any longer, not having exposed their true selves. Once they found Bill Spence didn't have the map in his safe, how much time would they take to search the entire town?

Then I had another thought. No one else in town knew Ranger Hanks was in with the gang, or Ike, for that matter. Ma and I were the only witnesses to that. Hanks could pretend he had a lawful reason to search the Lucky 7 Saloon safe and property. Ike could go back to the newspaper. The only ones stopping them was us. It was a chilling thought.

We waited. The sun hung lower and shadows stretched. The Widow lit a lamp in the kitchen. We all talked in low tones. The drummer, a man named Patterson, had a lot of entertaining stories to tell. A traveling man, he'd seen a lot of places I only ever dreamed about and witnessed a lot of amusing and strange things. The time flew.

It was pretty near dark when we heard a horse trotting toward the house. The horseman stopped a short distance away and hallooed.

The Widow opened the door a crack. "Halloo yourself," she said. "Who are you?"

"I'm travelin' through looking for lodging for the night. I heard tell you had room."

The voice sounded like one I'd heard. I glanced at Ma. She was listening intently.
"What's your name and business, stranger?" The Widow asked.

"Name's Bud, Bud Akins. I'm a salesman."

The widow looked at Patterson with a question on her face. Patterson shook his head, said he'd never heard of him, but I knew the voice. It was the skinny man who searched our house with the man Cherokee Bill. When I told the Widow, she didn't hesitate. She swung the door a bit wider and eased the barrel of the shotgun out.

"Mister, I got a 12 gauge says you need to climb off that horse slow and easy and shuck the gun you're carrying."

"Lady, I ain't done nothing to you. You got no call—"

"You ain't off that horse time I count five you are a dead man."

You could tell he was thinking hard about jerking the reins and making a run for it. He didn't know Widow McKenzie but maybe someone told him because after a couple of seconds he climbed down and pulled his pistol out slow and placed it in the dirt.

"Leave your horse be and come toward me," the Widow said.

Skinny man obeyed. He got just close enough for me to see his face when his head disappeared like a dandelion gone to seed when you blow on it. At about the same time we heard the boom that was the Sharps.

Nobody had to tell Widow McKenzie to get back inside and close the door.

Ma gasped. "Why would they do that to a friend?"

The Widow looked grim. "There's not much friendship among greedy men. I expect the shooter thought Bud would talk once we caught him, maybe tell their plans."

One of the hands, a man named Jim, thought as how the odds were evened up a bit now.
The Widow had already blown out the lamp. "That would be the Sharps rifle, like Johnny here was telling us. Don't anybody expose themselves to view. That man don't miss."

Ma asked, "Do you think they are all out there?"

"No way to tell," Jim said. "We got to assume they are."

"Three of 'em, far as we know," I said. "Ranger Hanks, Ike Sanders, and the guy with the Sharps."

Jim looked around. "Well, we got six of us who can pull a trigger." He glanced at the drummer, who was scrunched in a corner looking very white in the darkness. "Well, five, anyways."

The drummer waved a hand at us. "I'll be okay in a minute. I'm not used to this kind of thing."

Ma smiled at him. "None of us are."

We were all seated on the floor. Jim and the other hired hand, a man they called Shakes, was keeping watch through cracks in the shutters. We all had rifles or pistols, and each had an assigned window where we would station ourselves if there was an attack. Now there was nothing to do but wait.

"It might be the man with the Sharps is set up on that ridge just to keep us pinned in here until more of 'em come along," Jim said.

I'd been thinking about it. "Other thought is Ranger Hanks might be searching the Lucky 7 Saloon pretending to be legal like and Ike gone back to being a newspaper man in town. Who's to know? Long as we can't leave to tell anyone, they're safe enough."

"The man with the Sharps can't stay up there forever," Widow McKenzie said. "But they can't let you two disappear thinking you might go to where the map is hidden."

One part of the story we hadn't told anyone else was how the man with the Sharps had the map but didn't know it. But what the Widow said was true. The Sharps man could keep us pinned in the house until Ranger Hanks and Ike satisfied themselves the map couldn't be in Deep Water. That's when they'd ride out here. It began to look like a long night ahead.

CHAPTER FIFTEEN

Daylight faded outside like ice on a pond in spring, so slow you scarcely noticed. It was dark inside the Widow's kitchen sooner and our shapes became shadows and our faces blurred to each other. We made ourselves as comfortable as we could on the floor with blankets and cushions. The Widow kept the kitchen fire going on coals and found some beef and porridge to heat. I'd see her face clear as she bent to the fire to move the big fry pan around. The food was mighty tasty. I hadn't realized how hungry I'd become.

We kept a regular watch, but as the gloom deepened outside, I knew it wouldn't be long before there'd be nothing to see. That meant the killer could come a lot closer. That's when we'd have to rely on Scamp and his sharp ears.

We were all anxious and worried but determined. The drummer, though, was afraid. He kept talking as if the sound of his voice comforted him. We had to keep shushing him as the darkness grew so we could hear any noises outside the house.

"We have no chance," the drummer kept saying. "Those people can come right up to the house in the dark and we can't see to shoot them. We're all going to die."

"Now you shush up," the Widow ordered, finally. "If you keep talking like that, I'm the one you'll need to be scared of. I'll shoot you myself. Scamp here needs to be able to hear what's going on out there. He's a sight more valuable to me now than you are."

The Drummer stopped talking after that, but you could hear low moans come from his corner from time to time.

What the drummer had said got me to thinking, though. When it was true dark, after nightfall but before the moon rose, anyone could move about and not be seen, if they was careful. Maybe one of us could go outside and take a position to surprise the Sharps man. I slid over to talk to the Widow about it.

"That sounds like a good idea," she said. "It needs to be someone who can shoot good and see fairly well in the dark. Don't want someone shooting Tom if he comes back early for some reason. Jim or Shakes might do, but I don't think either of 'em done much shooting."

"It could be me," I said.

I couldn't see her face well, but I felt a squeeze on my arm. "I like that you offered," she said. "I expect your young eyes can see pretty good in the dark. But have you ever used a gun?"

I told her then about my practice sessions with Ike and how good I'd become. "I never shot anybody yet, but I know I can hit what I aim at."

I could see her shaking her head. "Your ma would plumb kill me."

"I'll tell her myself," I said. "Ma knows I've had to grow up right quick since the Kid came to town. We've both had to change and do things we don't like. She won't like this but she'll know I got to do it."

I was right about one thing—Ma sure didn't like it. She told me not to do it.

"You never shot anybody before," she said. "How do you know you won't hesitate and get killed? I don't want this for you, Johnny—to kill someone and have to live with it. This is not the life I wanted for you."

"Ma, nobody here has ever shot a man, but to stay alive we are gonna have to do it. You would do it if you were at the window and seen him running toward us. If I freeze up when I go to shoot, it's better to have just me get killed than find it out while trying to save you and the people here."

Ma didn't reply. I couldn't see her face clearly, but I knew the expression she'd be wearing, the one where my argument didn't deserve a response. Anyway, we both knew right from the beginning I was going to do it.

I waited for the Widow to decide the best time to leave. We figured the Sharps man would most likely be watching the door. There was no other door. All the windows were small, square and low to the ground. The Widow figured I could slide out the rear window in the bedroom. Once the inner door was shut, it should be too dark to see the shutters open. What we had to worry about was noise, not light.

I'd be lying to say I wasn't nervous. I checked the Navy Colt best I could in the dark. I filled the chamber Ike told me to keep empty. I thought I'd rather shoot myself in the leg climbing out the window than run out of bullets.

In the dark stillness, with just the drummer's occasional moaning, I had lots of thoughts. One was wondering how Ike could turn out the way he did. I'd seen him like a second pa, caring about me, teaching me valuable things, protecting me and Ma when all along he was wanting to find the map to the missing money. I wondered how long him and Ranger Hanks had been partnered up. Here Ike had talked about giving up his old ways but all the while he was waiting for his gang to get out of prison and come for the money. I guess the most valuable thing he taught me was not to trust even your best friend.

It seemed like hours had gone by when the Widow nudged me. I followed her to the bedroom. She went to the window and unlatched the shutter without a sound and peered through the crack before opening it wide. When she touched my shoulder, I took the Navy in my hand and wormed up and over the windowsill and eased down to the ground. I lay there for a spell, listening. I never heard the Widow close the shutters, she did it so quiet like.

It was lighter outside than I expected. I smelled sage and felt a soft breeze. I let my eyes adjust. I saw the nearest place for cover was a cottonwood tree maybe twenty yards away. I knew I needed to be in shadow by the time the moon rose. Already you could see a paleness in the night sky above the ridge that was the moonshine, so I didn't have much time. I began to Indian crawl toward the tree, flat on the ground, my pistol hand up front, just inches at a time. My face was turned away from the ridge where I figured Cherokee Bill to be so the light wouldn't pick up my pale skin. It was like being blind, not knowing what was happening in that direction. That was the scariest part.

By the time I reached the tree, I was sweaty, and my britches were full of dirt but by now there was shadow from the moon and I settled into the darkest part of it. I sat with my back against the trunk and the Navy Colt in my lap and waited and listened. Cicadas in the tree that had stopped their sound when I came close started up again in a while. Nothing else.

The moon rose higher and open places were brighter and shadowy places darker. If anyone came across one of those moonlit areas, I'd see him for sure. All I had to do now was stay still, stay awake and stay alert. None of that was easy.

I must have nodded off. I didn't know what woke me at first. Then I knew. The Cicadas had stopped their noise. That meant someone was close. Without moving anything else I let my eyes study what I could see. Nothing was different. I inched my head a tiny bit to my right and saw them, two coyotes ten feet away, ears pricked with curiosity, staring at me. Right when I was about to wave them away their heads swiveled to look toward the ridge. A moment later they were gone like ghosts.

Looking that way, I could see nothing. The moon sat above the ridge its brilliance obliterated everything beneath it. But my ears heard what had alarmed the coyotes—hoofs on turf. Measured, not a gallop. No way to tell if they were coming or going. They stopped or faded—I couldn't tell. Maybe Cherokee Bill had gone away or maybe somebody had joined him.

Four men had left me and ma at our house and rode to town to look for the map—Ranger Hanks, Ike, Cherokee Bill and the skinny man named Bud. Now Bud lay dead outside the ranch house. Were there more? There was no way to know but I didn't think so. I figured the whole gang was at our house because nobody would trust Ike and Hanks not to make off with the money if they had found it. If the hoof sounds I had just heard was someone coming from town to help Cherokee Bill, it had to be either Ranger Hanks or Ike. More likely, though, what I'd heard was the Cherokee Bill headed back to town because he couldn't see anything to shoot.

I sat there a good while longer and watched and waited but didn't see or hear anything. It made sense to me that he might ride back to town figuring we were as good as trapped in the house and would keep until morning. He'd be right unless I proved him wrong.

My heart beat hard just thinking about getting up and walking up to the ridge. It was a big chance to take but the darkness was my friend now and I was pretty sure Sharps man had gone. My impulse was to run from cover to cover but I figured moving slow was better because slow is harder to see in the dark. At least, I hoped so.

The moon was high now, round and bright. I could see high chaparral and trees like bunched darkness and moved in and out of those shadows. I moved just my feet, kept my upper half still with my arms to the side and concentrated on stepping slow and quiet. It took a long time to get up on the ridge.

The ridge top was mostly tall grasses and short brush. The moon shone bright all along it. Nobody was there. I found where a man had been for a long while, flattening the grass. Stamped down grass downslope showed where his horse had stood. Cherokee Bill likely did not intend to return tonight but I didn't know for sure. One thing, I could wait right here and get the drop on him if he did come back. But if more than one of them came, I would be in trouble.

I sat down right there to think about it. I thought about the map wrapped around the Bowie knife, wondering if any of the men would think to look at it. I guessed that the Cherokee hadn't had time to open it and study his new treasure since he must have come right out here from town and sat in the dark. Maybe he would take a look at it back in town, if that's where they were.

But what I knew about Ike, he wouldn't like that Cherokee Bill left us this way. Ike paid attention to every detail. He'd think someone should be guarding in case we made a run for it, which even if you couldn't see you could hear. He'd insist someone come back here right away. Earliest, someone could be back here was another hour.

How fast could the foreman Tom get back with the law? Not knowing where he was headed, I couldn't answer that. But the nearest law I knew about was two days or more. I figured we were pretty much on our own. We were up against experienced killers. I'd seen what Cherokee Bill could do with his rifle. I'd seen Ranger

Hanks shoot down a man without a thought. And Ike was the one who taught me how to shoot.

We had numbers, but little experience. I figured Widow McKenzie maybe would be the best of us from defending her home over the years. And ma could shoot. But the women were best suited to defending the house with rifles instead of running around in the brush. I figured Jim would be helpful even if he hadn't done much shooting. Shakes, maybe, too. But Tom was out of the picture now and the drummer wouldn't do nobody any good. Then there was me and I never shot anybody before even though I could shoot.

There it was. We were five guns to their three, but I had to give them the odds. We needed a plan.

CHAPTER SIXTEEN

Widow McKenzie let me in through the door and everybody gathered around the kitchen table. I told what happened and how I figured we had an hour to come up with a plan.

"We got one thing in our favor, the way I see it," I said. "I know Ike and how he thinks, meaning someone will be back to that ridge soon to keep an eye on us. Maybe just the Indian with the Sharps or maybe Ike with him or maybe all three. But I'm hoping it's just Cherokee Bill. Any which way, we got to keep them from boxing us in. So, we'll set a trap."

I looked at the Widow. "I figure you and Ma and Scamp is all that's needed to keep them away from the house so long as it's dark."

She nodded.

"Me and Jim and Shakes will go back to the ridge, find us a good ambush spot, and wait." I looked at Jim and Shakes. They both nodded, though maybe not so cheerful as could be.

We all looked at the drummer. He avoided our eyes.

Jim said, "When?"

I said, "Right now, before they come back."

We walked out the door and hiked right on up to the ridge figuring speed was better than caution right then. Dark as it was, the moon shed enough light for us to find good places to defend, hidden by rocks and chaparral just the far side of the ridge near where Cherokee Bill had been. I figured him to return to the same place having sighted in his rifle from there already.

Then we waited.

We waited so long I had begun to think I'd been wrong about the whole idea. It was hard to tell how much time was passing. The moon was still high but edged away from behind the ridge and hung more in the center of the sky like a big barn lantern. I could hear cicadas in the trees off a ways and occasional rustling around in the leaves from night creatures. An owl was hunting somewhere to the east and you could hear the soft "who-o-o" from time to time. There was more of a breeze up here on the ridge, but it was warmish. I was tempted to call softly to Jim and Shakes to see how they was doing, but I didn't. I hoped they wouldn't either. But it did feel lonely.

My mind took me places I wished it wouldn't, like how nice it had been before all this happened, how comfortable and safe seeming our home was, how good it had felt to work for Ike and be responsible and earn a wage and learn a trade. Now this. Nothing was the same anymore and I felt alone and betrayed and like my life was now just moment to moment.

When the horse hooves came, I heard them right away, even as soft as they was on the turf. They came straight toward where we were hiding. I got up to a squat as quiet as I could, but my knees didn't like it and cracked so loud they sounded like branches snapping to me. But the hooves kept coming.

Then they stopped.

I held my breath. It sounded like one horse, but it was hard to know for sure. The hooves stopped too soon. If the rider stayed where he was, it was too far from our ambush and it would fail. We waited. After a long spell the hooves sounded again, and right after that the shadowy form of horse and rider appeared in the moonlit grass in front of me.

The horse stopped but the rider didn't get down. Instead, a voice spoke.

"Johnny, I know you are here." It was Ike.

I didn't say anything, just listened.

"Johnny, I had to play along, you know."

I stepped out with the Navy Colt pointed at him. "Climb down, Ike. Do it with one hand in the air. You know I won't miss from here."

He did, slow and easy. When he was standing by his horse, I made him pull the Colt with two fingers with the other hand still in the air and toss it to me, which he did. I saw his rifle in the scabbard on his horse. I figured his coat pocket was full of shells.

"Where's your man with the Sharps?" I asked.

"You mean Cherokee Bill? He's fast asleep back in town, I reckon."

I made him sit. "Why are you here?"

He sat cross-legged looking cool in the moonlight like he was about to have tea. "I needed to talk with you, Johnny, while the others are elsewhere."

"How'd you know I'd be here?"

"I didn't, but I'm not surprised."

"My guess is you really came here to make certain we stayed trapped in the ranch house until morning."

He nodded. "That would make sense except it isn't true."

I stared at Ike. I felt a lot of anger build up in me. "I don't know what is true with you anymore, Ike."

Ike was silent for a moment. "Can't say I blame you, Johnny, from the way things look. But the fact is I had to go along with Hanks and my old gang or die. Dead, I'd be no help to you."

"Keep talking."

"Johnny, fact is it's true I come to Deep Water lookin' for the robbery money. I figured your pa knew where it was. When I got here, I found your pa was dead and your ma was a widow with a young boy. I decided to take up quarters in the Lucky 7 Saloon for a spell and get the lay of the land. I found out pretty quick your ma didn't have much money, not living the way she was, doing odd jobs like helping in the saloon and selling the goats' milk. If she had the money, the two of you would have been living high. So that meant either your pa never did take the money, or he never told your ma he had it."

"Why would he do that?" I asked.

"Well, that's the question, isn't it? Was he holding out for a rainy day or was the money maybe too difficult to go get or did he not want your ma to know what he had done? I figured it could be any one of those reasons. Then your pa gets killed sudden and never has the chance to tell your ma about the money, even if he had it." Ike looked at me, like he was watching for my response.

I said nothing.

"As I watched your ma living her life, taking care to raise you proper, I got to admiring her. She made me take a hard look at my own life. Seems the longer I stayed in Deep Water and watched the folks there and how happy in their lives everyone looked, the bigger the itch grew in me to turn my own life around and do something meaningful." He paused, looked at me. "You know the rest. I'd done some journalism and printing as a young man. Deep Water didn't have a newspaper and I knew I could build one and that seemed a good thing to do."

"Maybe just to impress my ma and to get close to me," I said.

Ike grinned. "None of that hurt, for sure, but it wasn't my real reason. My gang was scattered. It was the first time I'd been on my own in a long while, able to think my own thoughts rather than let others take me to places greedy men wanted to go. I wanted to be a different person."

"And now?"

"My gang drifted back from prison or wherever they'd been over the years. They never forgot the money that was snatched out from under their noses. They wanted it and they wanted revenge for losing it. They thought if they found me, they'd likely find the money."

"They was almost right," I said. "Sit tight." I glanced toward the shadows. "Jim, Shakes, come take away Mr. Sanders' weapons. He's coming with us to the ranch house."

Ike didn't seem surprised when the two men came out of hiding. He watched them approach, then said, "You don't want to do this."

"Why not?"

"Because I can help you better from inside the gang than if you take me prisoner."

I shook my head. "I got to trust you first, and I'm a long spell from there. Besides, once we got you out of the way you only got two men left. I figure we can handle that, even if they are gunfighters."

Ike shook his head. "You're wrong, Johnny. There's more than two. I told you more was coming."

Jim and Shakes had taken Ike's Colt and the rifle and stood there watching.

"How many more?" I asked.

"Two more last night. They'd have come with me now except they don't trust Ranger Hanks and wanted to keep an eye on him while Bill slept."

"Is that the whole of it?" I asked. I didn't trust Ike about this either, but I wanted him to spin out his entire story.

"There might be more, depending on whether the rumors sayin' they died are true."

Jim spoke up. "What guarantee have we got you are with us and not with Hanks and Ben?"

Ike looked at him. "None I can think of, other than I think I believe Johnny here knows I'd never hurt him or his ma."

I scoffed. "Why should I ever believe that when your man with the Sharps been riddling the house with me and Ma in it?"

Ike shook his head once, slow. "I didn't want that, boy, but I couldn't stop it without giving myself away. I just hoped you'd keep your heads down."

Shakes spoke up. "He's lying. We got one of them. That's one less we got to fight."

Ike stared at him, kinda taking his measure. "If you leave me loose, you might not have to fight anybody." He looked at me. "Think about it this way, Johnny. Either I been lying about everything all along or I'm not lying now. You got to decide which you believe."

It was a whole lot to think about. Years spent with Ike, day after day, trusting and believing in him. And Ma, too, even though he annoyed her from time to time. It was a lot to throw away.

Then Ike said something that changed everything.

"You're forgetting something, Johnny," he said. "You're forgetting the Kid. He's still out there and he still means us harm. All of us."

CHAPTER SEVENTEEN

I let him go. You could tell Jim and Shakes thought it was a big mistake. In their minds it was simple math, one from three leaves just two. Yet Ike had said two more gang members were with them now. Like he told me, either he's lying about everything, or nothing.

What I hadn't told Ike was Tom had ridden off to bring back the law. Maybe it didn't matter if I had because no one knew how long it would take. But to us it meant an end to things somewhere in the future and that was a relief, even if a small one.

It seemed he still didn't know about the map, otherwise he wouldn't have come. That meant either Bill hadn't seen it or he was keeping it to himself. I thought how none of this would be happening if they knew they had the map. They'd all ride out to look for the money. But two things had stopped me from telling Ike. One, they might think the map was a fake we'd made ourselves just to get rid of them. The other thing was this feeling that if pa did hide away the money, why should they have it?

Jim and I walked back down to the house. We left Shakes up there in case Ike doubled back. I didn't think he would. The fact is once I decided to believe Ike's story, I knew I had to swallow the whole package, whatever happened.

What I wasn't gonna do was see other folks hurt by my decision. Back at the house I told everyone about my meeting with Ike and how I decided to believe him. The Widow just looked at me and nodded like she was ready to accept my decision.

Ma wasn't happy. "Johnny, how can you trust him? Look what he's done to you. He's got this crazy gunman trying to kill you, he's got you studying to be a gunfighter yourself and next we know he's riding with his old gang and that sneaky ranger. And they are trying to kill us. What does he have to do to make you see his true self? Johnny, he's playing you like some old fiddle."

"Ma, you might be right, but I had to make up my own mind. But no one should suffer for it if I'm wrong. What's done is done. We need to plan what to do next. First thing is, we can't let ourselves be pinned down in this house again."

We talked about it then. The Widow made some strong coffee and baked up some biscuits which were mighty good. The drummer decided as how he'd had enough for one night and left to saddle up and move on. We wished him well.

Shakes came down after about an hour. He said Ike hadn't returned and no one else came along. We had about another hour to daylight. We were pretty sure they'd be coming back then.
The Widow's idea was to defend the house with a crossfire. She and Ma would remain in the house with rifles. Shakes and Jim would find cover at the barn or bunkhouse where they had a line of fire that covered the house. They'd hold their fire until the gang came close to the house and try to catch them in between. I would be the wild card and hang back hidden near the ridge and watch to see what they did. I took a canteen of water, several biscuits, and a rifle, said bye to Ma and walked back up the hill.

I hid in a different place, expecting Ike would avoid where we hid last night. But I was wrong. When they came an hour later, they came to exactly the same place. To me that meant Ike hadn't told them about us capturing him. There were five of them, which meant Ike wasn't lying about two more gang members, either.

From where I was hiding on the back side of the ridge, I could just see them gathered at the spot where Cherokee Bill had kept us pinned with the Sharps. They all stayed on horseback, talking. Sometimes I'd hear a voice loud, like they was arguing. Then everyone would get quiet and I would hear Ranger Hanks' voice talkin' low, but too far away to get the words. It sure seemed like he was the man in charge now.

When they rode off, one man stayed and dismounted. Two rode one way along the ridge and two rode my way. The ones who came past me were Ranger Hanks and another man I didn't recognize. I figured they were thinking to come at the house from two sides, maybe riding hard at it or maybe find cover and shoot it up. That meant the other two might fall into our trap.

I had to find out who the man was who stayed on the ridge and what he was doing. I worked my way around behind him as quiet as I could using cover, then worked toward him. He had a rifle and was setting up to shoot from a prone position. I couldn't see his face but figured it must be Cherokee Bill with the Sharps. I let him get good and settled, nestled up with his cheek against the stock, the barrel laid out across the rocks he'd set up for himself. Once he was all stretched out, I made my move and rushed up the hill from behind with the Navy Colt in my hand.

Bill couldn't hardly move, flat on his stomach as he was with no idea anyone might come from behind him. He tried to twist around at first but realized it was hopeless and stopped. He didn't let go of the rifle, though. He tried to talk me down like I was just some kid.

"Come, boy, put down the gun. I will not shoot you. You can't shoot me, you don't have the stomach."

The whole time he was talking he kept edging that big rifle around trying to get the barrel end pointed at me. He had a pistol in a holster at his waist but couldn't draw it while lying on his stomach, and the funny thing was the more he kept rolling himself around with the Sharps the more he buried the pistol. But all I saw was the huge barrel of that Sharps.

I don't know why I didn't shoot. I knew he wasn't gonna stop trying to get that rifle around and pointed at me. He really didn't think I'd shoot him. Maybe he was right that I really wasn't able to shoot a man that way, lying down in front of me, defenseless. But he got the barrel a good way around while I hesitated. Then in one sudden motion, he rolled the rest of the way and fired.

My instincts were good, and my reaction was fast. I stepped sideways and pulled the trigger at the same time. His rifle was so loud it sounded like I was next to a cannon. I even heard the whistle of the bullet passing my ear. I never heard my gun go off, but the bullet went through his head. He slumped down and never moved.

Funny thing, I'd just shot someone for the first time but wasn't even thinking about that right away. Instead I was wondering how soon the others would come running back up to investigate. I was already reloading the Navy out of habit and ready to cock back the hammer for my next shot. But no one came.

I guess the two shots must have come so close together the big boom of the Sharps hid the sound of my pistol. The gang below likely thought Cherokee Bill was shooting at the house like they planned. That gave me the idea to pretend I was him. I pried the Sharps from his hand and lay it on the ground. I got on my knees and pushed both hands against his side and rolled him over, away from his rifle nest. It wasn't easy. Cherokee Bill was a big man.

It was while touching him, his body still warm like he was sleeping there, that what I'd done began to bother me. There was blood where his head had been, I had to scrape it away not to lie in it. My stomach wasn't very steady, but I had a job to do, so I ignored it.

I'd never practiced with a rifle. I never even seen a Sharps up close until now. I looked at the breech and saw there was a brass cartridge in it. I tried to take it out. A little metal piece had it blocked but I figured out how to move it away and then I tipped out the brass, still hot from the shot. Bill had a leather pouch slung around his neck. Inside it I found a half dozen large cartridges with the biggest bullets I'd ever seen. I pulled the pouch over his head and lay it open next to me. I took a cartridge out and slid it into the breech, pushed closed the blocker piece, and pulled back the hammer.

All was quiet below. From here on the ridge I could see the house and the front of the bunkhouse, the rear of it hidden by a large tree. It took a while to find the attackers. I waited until I saw movement from the east side of the house where Hanks and the other outlaw were hidden, just small figures from where I watched. They were on foot. I figure they'd hidden the horses in the tree grove somewhere.

I heard shots. They seemed to come from the bunkhouse side of the ranch house. I saw a figure firing at the house from behind a woodpile. I couldn't see the other one. After they started shooting the men on Hanks' side began firing. Rifle fire came from the house. The battle had begun. There was a great confusion of shots sounding. I saw the figure at the woodpile stand suddenly, half turn, and then fall. I figured he'd been shot from the bunk house. I couldn't see the other bandit, couldn't tell what happened to him.

The figures on Hank's side of the house started to creep forward, shooting as they came. It seemed like there was less return fire from the house. It was up to me now.

I nestled the Sharps against my shoulder and my cheek and looked through the sight at one of the figures. I aimed low, so I wouldn't overshoot. When the figure was still for a moment, I pulled the trigger. The rifle acted like a live thing. It kicked back at me, almost jumped out of my hands. Somehow my jaw got hit like a punch from a boxer. I was stunned for a moment. When I could look again, I saw the figure I'd aimed at was lying on the ground. No other figures were in sight. No more shots sounded. After a long while I heard a galloping horse.

I waited, watched both sides of the house, saw nothing moving. After a while a hat appeared at the bunk house door, like someone was peering out. It went back in, then someone stepped out, hiding from me, worried about the Sharps, likely. No shots sounded. I guessed the battle was over.

I stood, checked my load in the rifle, reloaded the Sharps and slid the ammo purse over my head. But before I walked away, I looked under Bill's coat. Sure enough, the bowie knife was there, tucked into his belt still wrapped in the leather. I took it, slid it under my own belt and with the rifle and the Sharps like two lead pipes in the crook of my arm, descended the long ridge toward the house. By the time I was halfway there the men from the bunkhouse were standing in the yard watching me. As I arrived the women came out from the house.

Ma came right over to me to be sure I wasn't hurt. She saw the swelling on my jaw and gave me a concerned look.

"Don't worry, Ma. That came from the Sharps rifle. That man Cherokee Bill is dead."

Those were the first words spoken among us and left an empty, dread reaction now that we all had time to feel what we'd just been through. For me it was a man dead by my hand, up close and personal. Everyone seemed to look at me different.

115

Jim walked to the woodpile, knelt by the man lying there. "He's dead," he said. He stood, looked at Shakes. "Shakes here was the one who shot him." We all looked at Shakes curiously, then walked over to the woodpile. None of us recognized the man. He was dead, all right, shot through the neck with a rifle bullet.

"I think there is one more on the other side of the house," the Widow said. "I saw him fall but I don't know how bad it was."

I figured she was talking about the one I hit with the Sharps. We walked around to the other side of the house. We were a somber group. We were still on edge, alert. Any strange noise made us bring up our rifles. It was a strange feeling of triumph and yet regret. We found the body of the third man part way to the trees at the back of the house. His head was a mess. I'd tried to aim low, but it almost wasn't enough. I was lucky or maybe this fella was unlucky. None of us recognized him, either. We figured both dead men for the newly arrived robbers.

The Widow was adding it up. "The only ones left from the whole gang are Ike Sanders and Ranger Hanks." She sighed, looked at the dead man. "There ain't no law we can call out here this time. Just the undertaker."

"I don't fancy any of us riding into town until we know what Hanks and Sanders will do," Jim said.

"You're right," the Widow said. She looked at Shakes. "How many shovels we got? Let's put 'em in the ground."

We did. It was a sad task, and we worked in silence. We decided to bury all three up on the ridge. It would be a nice view from there, but we also figured the three graves might come as a warning to anyone else thinking to attack us. Jim fashioned the crosses. We harnessed a horse to the wagon and lay the two strangers on it and hauled them up the hill. Right where Cherokee Bill lay was an area of soft earth and the men took turns digging three graves with the two shovels Shakes found. It took us much of the rest of the day.

The Widow and Ma insisted on singing and saying a few words over them. We were polite but it seemed hard to pray over strangers who done their best to kill us.

CHAPTER EIGHTEEN

We gathered around the big kitchen table in the ranch house and drank hot tea and finished off the rest of the biscuits. The Widow even had a bottle of schnapps to touch up the tea to perk us up. We were beyond tired from being up all night constantly on the alert with the intense emotion that comes from fighting to stay alive. We all needed sleep.

"Do you think they'll be back?" Ma asked.

"Not soon, anyway," the Widow said. "Just two men ain't going to defeat us where five couldn't."

"Think there's more of the gang coming?" Jim was pouring out a drop more of the Dr. McGillicud. He didn't seem to mind the idea of more fighting.

I shook my head. "I think any gang members who are still alive and wanted some of that stolen money would've come here by now." I ticked them off on my fingers. "There's the first two, Pernelli and O'Brien that Hanks killed. Then you got these three we just killed. That's five right there. Add Ike and that's a pretty good size gang."

"We just can't be certain," Ma said.

We were all silent for a time, thinking about it.

"We can't always be looking over our shoulders," Jim said. "We got to sleep some time."

Widow McKenzie had been at the stove cooking up more food. Now she turned and spoke up. "My thinking is Ranger Hanks and Ike Sanders will lay low for a bit. They must figure the law will be coming sooner or later. If I was them, I'd go back to rangering and newspaper writing like nothing happened and act like I didn't know anything about what happened out here. They don't want to rile up the townspeople if they haven't already. They'll wait to see what we do next."

"Ike Sanders was saying he's on our side," Shakes said.

"If you believe him," Jim added.

"I don't think either of them will quit until they get what they came for," the Widow said.

I figured she was right. Even if Tom got back with a lawman, we couldn't prove either Hanks or Ike was here shooting at us. True, we'd caught Ike up on the ridge, but even then, he was saying he was with us, not against us. We saw him ride away. We had no way to prove he ever came back.

There was only one way out of this I could see. I didn't like it and I knew Ma wasn't going to like it, but it had to be done. I stood up to say my piece.

"Hanks and Ike ain't going to give up until they get what they came for, like Ms. McKenzie says. They think me and Ma know where the money is, that's why they keep coming at us. If I go away, they'll follow me and leave you alone. They'll think I know where it's hid, think I went to get it. They'll both follow me because they don't trust each other. Simple as that."

No one liked the idea.

"That ain't right," the Widow said. "We don't need a young boy with all his life in front of him to protect us by going off and getting himself killed. We outnumber them, we got the law on our side. We'll be fine."

"She's right," Jim said. "We already beat them once and if needs be, we can do it again."

"At least until Tom comes back with the law," the Widow said.

Heads nodded all around the table.

I felt almost like crying, from how they acted. Just a day ago, I didn't even know two of them and now they felt like brothers to me. I guess when you risk your life together with people, you grow close like that. It was a good feeling, but I still knew it wasn't the answer.

They weren't going to let me go, though, I could see that, so I shrugged and acted like they convinced me.

We made a meal of the soup Widow McKenzie cooked up but most of us were nodding our heads even as we ate. We spoke about the next day. The Widow wanted Ma and me to move in for a while. She had it all figured out to send Shakes and Jim with the wagon for anything we needed and Scamp along with them to drive the goats back here to the ranch.

"Let them search your place for the money to their hearts content," she said. "Maybe after they dig up the goat yard and the garden, they'll convince themselves there ain't no money."

I could see Ma was sad about deserting the place pa built for us.

"It's only for a little while, Ma," I said. I wanted to convince her because I wanted her safe here while I was gone. We all got set for some sleep even though it was still early in the day. The Widow found blankets and big coats for us all to lie on. Shakes was already snoring in a corner.

I told the Widow I'd take first watch. I figured to watch from the barn, out of sight.

She agreed reluctantly. "Johnny, you need sleep too. Just watch an hour or so and come get me. Promise?"

I promised.

But what I did was wait until I figured everyone was asleep, saddle up my horse, and walk the horse until I was out of hearing. Then I mounted up and rode off.

I didn't have a clear idea where to go. At the ranch gate the choice was go south back toward town or north up toward Indian Territory. My whole plan was to get Hanks and Ike to think I had a map and was headed off to get the money, so they'd follow me. But if I rode right through town in broad daylight and someone saw me, Ike or Hanks might figure out I was trying to trick them or worse, might try to stop me. Yet if I just rode off and nobody knew to follow me, what good would that do?

Then I thought of Meghan Kline, the cute red-headed girl. Her family lived on the road north of town. The sun was high, it being near noon. She might just be on the porch about now. I rode there to find out. She wasn't on the porch, but she was in the front yard tending some flowers. I rode up to the fence. She looked up and smiled.

"Hi, Johnny."

"Hi, Meghan." I was trying to put together some words to tell her. I suppose I'm shy, when it gets right down to it, at least around girls. I wanted to say something about how I was leaving but once I was there looking at her, I couldn't think what to say.

"I was sorry to hear about the trouble you and your Ma been having," she said. "There's bad men around. I'm thankful we got Ranger Hanks in town to watch over things now."

Well, now I really didn't know what to say. I hated that she thought Hanks was a good, lawful man. I supposed the whole town thought that way. I swallowed my pride and played along.

"Thanks, Meghan. I guess that's good. I like knowing you'll be safe cause I got to go away for a while."

Right off she looked sad and that made me feel better.

"Will you be gone long?"

"I can't rightly say. It's something I got to do."

She looked hard at me like she was trying to figure me out. "Is it far?"

"It's pretty far, I expect," I said. She didn't say anything, and I waited. The quiet got uncomfortable so I reined my horse around and said, "I'll see you when I get back." I rode off, thinking how stupid that sounded.

I was mad at myself but felt something warm in me thinking she looked sad because I was going away. I rode back north, away from town. I expected she'd probably tell her Ma or her dad I'd said I was going and sooner or later word would get to Ike or Hanks. I figured I probably had a few hours before they came after me.

I let my horse ease into a trot and followed the road north. After I passed the Box Elder Ranch gate it was about ten miles to turnoff for the Fort Worth road. I'd figure which way to go once I got there.

The sun was hot on my back and the warm breeze didn't help and I began sweating. It was flat open range all around with just a few stands of cottonwoods here and there, mostly far over to the east where the river ran. The dust was thick on the road and kicked up as we trotted along.

On hot days like this sometimes you'd see what looked like lakes on the horizon or trees that weren't really there. When I saw a horse in the shimmering distance with no rider, I figured it must be a mirage. I didn't think much of it.

After a while, though, the horse was still there, not moving. As I came closer, I saw it was grazing at the side of the road, its reins trailing. When I came up on it, I could see dried sweat on its flanks like it had been run hard. It was saddled with a rifle in the scabbard but no rider. Then I saw the Box Elder brand on it and got a real bad feeling.

There was no one around anywhere. I watered the horse from my water skin and looked it over and didn't see any injury. I remounted and took its reins and it came along with me fine. I figured it had to be Tom's horse. Question was, what happened to Tom? The other question in my mind was did whatever happened to Tom happen on his way to Fort Worth or on his way back?

It was when I reached the road intersection for Fort Worth, I got my answer. The roads met in a small grove of cottonwoods. It was a pretty place, with green grass and a small stream bed under a high cut bank. There were several pools of water with skitter bugs on them. I let the horses drink and stretched my legs. The Fort Worth road followed the stream bed on the high side of the bank traveling east and west while my road went on north out into the flatland toward Indian Territory. I walked it a short way. It was overgrown some, less traveled from here on. I turned back and as I neared the trees, I heard flies buzzing and that's when I saw Tom. He was hanging from a thick cottonwood branch. He'd been hanging there a while.

There would be no law coming back to Deep Water to help us.

CHAPTER NINETEEN

It took me most of the afternoon to cut Tom down and tie him across the saddle of his horse. Tom was a big man, much bigger than me. The only way I knew to get him on his horse was to lower him to it by the hanging rope which the killers had flung over the limb and tied off to the trunk. The horse was skittish, naturally, so I had to hobble it right there and blindfold it, then take a turn with the end of the rope around the trunk to help me lower Tom. As soon as his boots touched the horse's back it would startle and move. That's mainly why it took me so long.

Finding Tom changed my plans. I couldn't just leave him there and go on. I had to take him back to the Box Elder Ranch and see how Widow McKenzie wanted to handle things. Once I had Tom laid across the saddle and tied down so he wouldn't slip off I mounted up and set off back toward the ranch, leading his horse.

It was near nightfall. I had a notion I might meet Ike or Hanks if they had heard I was leaving and decided to follow me, so when I rounded a bend and came face to face with Hanks, I wasn't all that surprised. He was, though. His eyebrows shot way up and he pulled up directly in front of me.

"Why, hello, Johnny," he said. "What have you got there?"

"I figure you already know," I said.

"Well no, I don't. Looks to me like a man's body. Is he injured or dead?"

"I found him hanging by the neck from a cottonwood limb back at the junction," I said. "He's pretty much dead."

"You gonna tell me who he is?"

"I figure you already know that, too," I said.

Hanks sighed. "Fact is, I don't. I'd appreciate it if you told me."

I stared at him. "This here is Tom Fedlow, Widow McKenzie's ranch foreman. Somebody caught and hung him so's he couldn't bring lawful help back to Deep Water."

"We already got law in Deep Water," Hanks said. "I'm the law."

I didn't even answer. By this time his game was just plain silly.

"Where're you taking him?" Hanks asked.

"Back to the ranch," I said. "Let Widow McKenzie take care of him."

"I think we should ride back to town with him and take him to the undertaker and treat this lawful like," he said.

I shook my head. "I plan to let the Widow McKenzie decide."

I waited, a little afraid of what Hanks might decide to do next. I'd seen him shoot a man as casually as some people pour tea. But I felt like I had to stand my ground.

Hanks didn't answer. He just stared at me, but I could see his jaw twitch. "What brought you out this way in the first place?" he asked.

"I came to see what was taking Tom so long. Now I know."

He chewed on that.

Before he could say anything else, I asked, "What brings you out this way?"

He stared at me, then he laughed. "Johnny, you are special. Which makes it kind of sad that I'll likely have to shoot you one day." With that, he wheeled his horse around and headed back toward Deep Water at a fast trot.

To tell the truth, I was relieved. I didn't want to have to try to draw on him while on horseback. I'd never tried that before. Fact is, I'd never drawn on anyone before and drawing against Ranger Hanks

125

while on horseback didn't seem like a good way to start out. By now I'd come to realize the ranger liked to pick his own times to draw.

I rode on. It was slow going. Tom's horse didn't like what he was carrying and wasn't used to being led. My right arm got mighty achy. Each time we came to thick brush or a tree grove I studied it extra careful. I didn't see Hanks as an ambusher or back shooter but someone else might have come out part of the way with him. You never know.

It was dusk when I arrived at the ranch. When I rode past the bunk house Shakes came out with his rifle on his shoulder. I was glad to see they were keeping watch. At the main house Ma and the widow were the first to come out. Ma seemed just happy to see me, but the widow went right to Tom where he lay over his saddle. She didn't cry or anything like that, but you could see maybe she wanted to. Jim came looking sleepy and we all took Tom down and carried him into the bunk house and laid him out on a bunk. While I was in the barn, I heard familiar voices and was happy to see our goats in a nice big stall. They seemed pleased to see me.

We stood there looking down at Tom. Ma and the Widow set about cleaning him up and getting him a change of clothes from his duffle for burial. Jim and Shakes were mad and upset and cursed Ike and Hanks up and down. They wanted to go settle matters right then.

I'd been going over things in my mind, though. I'd begun to think Hanks wasn't part of the hanging. His surprise when he met me seemed real and when he asked who was slung over the horse it seemed like he truly didn't know.

"Tom hung from that tree a long time," I said. "Somebody must have caught him right when he left here last night. But we know Ike and Hanks and the rest were all still in town. They couldn't ride back to our house, find us missing, then track us out here and still catch up to Tom. He left pretty much right when Ma and me got here."

The widow looked closely at me. "Who could have done this to Tom, then? You don't think it was just some robber happened along? Tom didn't have anything of value with him except his horse and saddle and they didn't take them."

I could tell Ma was looking at me, not liking what she was hearing. I didn't look at her.

I shook my head. "There's one other man wouldn't want the law coming here right now."

Ma whispered, "The Kid."

Jim and Shakes looked confused.

"Is the Kid riding with Ike and Hanks?" Shakes asked.

"I don't figure he's riding with anyone but his own self. Ike told me the Kid came here for revenge on Ike because he thinks Ike killed his dad years ago. Ike says he didn't do it, but..." I shrugged.

Jim was puzzling things out. "Ike told us last night he wasn't really on Ranger Hanks side, just pretending to be to keep you and your Ma safe."

Ma turned her head quickly at that. It was the first she'd heard it.

Jim was still chewing on things. "And you say the Kid ain't with either of them. But I heard the Kid wanted to shoot it out with you."
"It was Ike he wanted," I said. "He was trying to use me to get to Ike."

Ma tried to explain it all. "There was a robbery back before the war. Robbers stole the Wells Fargo box from a stagecoach. My husband Sage was a Texas Ranger back then and was a passenger. Sage went after the gang, killed one, captured all the others but Ike, who was the leader. The money disappeared. Ike and Ranger Hanks think my husband took it and hid it. Ike came to Deep Water when Johnny there was just a tyke and stayed. He started the newspaper and hired Johnny on just to learn where the money was hidden. The Kid learned Ike was here and came for revenge. When the gang members got out of jail, they came looking for Ike and the money.

127

Ranger Hanks came for the money too. I guess they all joined up somehow."

"Seems like the only thing they got in common is bothering you folks," the widow said.

"They can't let go of the idea that pa didn't have the money."

"Well, they been stirring up the wrong people. Now they killed Tom, who's like family to me. After we bury him proper, I think we'll sort things out." With that veiled threat, the widow went back to work with Ma to make Tom as presentable as possible.

I was mighty hungry not having eaten since the widow's left-over biscuits. Jim and Shakes were taking care of my horse and the one Tom rode, so I left the barn for the kitchen. I found some bread and a new cheese and set about eating my fill. While I ate, I thought about what the Kid did to Tom and what that meant. I figured he had a plan and didn't want the law or any other folks coming to Deep Water to mess it up. Things was working out well for him. Ike's old gang was mostly dead now. If Ike wasn't lying, he was on his own.

Then I thought the Kid could be thinking Ike had turned against Ma and me, seeing the way he'd been siding with Ranger Hanks and pursuing us. Maybe the Kid would figure by hurting Ma or me he'd only be helping Ike and leave off doing that.

Maybe.

After I ate my fill, I needed sleep. The blankets and coats we'd used for bedding were still along the walls, so I made a nest of several and went right off to sleep.

I woke to someone gently nudging my arm. It was Shakes. It was full dark, and I could see his face only from the moonglow through the window. He was apologetic.

"I know you need sleep real bad. We all done watches tonight and we left yours for last. We got about two hours to first light."

I rubbed my eyes and tried to get my brain working, then nodded. I could see black lumps of people sleeping here and there. He handed me the Sharps and the ammo purse. I had fallen asleep with the Navy Colt at my side, so I slid it into the holster and cracked the door and slipped outside. I waited up against the wall of the house for my eyes to adjust. The moon was low and would be gone soon.

I walked up the hill to the ridge to take my watch. Now that I had some food in me and had got some sleep, I felt pretty good, but I still moved slow to blend into the night. I found a spot on the ridgetop where I could see down on the buildings but also see toward the road where someone might come. I settled in.

The dawn came gentle, just a glow in the east painting pink and red sky, then fingers of light reaching toward me on the ridge. Once they were on me their warmth felt good, even though the night hadn't been very cold. I basked in the sunlight a while before going down to the house.

When I stepped inside, only the widow was on her feet. She was firing up the stove. The room was still chilled from the night and felt damp. I rested the Sharps against the wall and sat down at the table nearest the fire. The widow smiled at me but didn't say anything so as not to wake the others. She was heating water and I was real interested in a cup of something hot.

Folks began to stir. Ma was first rising. She came over and gave me a big hug, all warm and smelling of lavender soap. She smiled and stepped outside to take care of her morning needs.

The outhouse was around back, and the tub fed by the spring was up against the house wall at the corner. We heard her steps go around the side of the house. Others were stirring by now and speaking softly. The water was boiling on the stove and the widow was laying out bacon in the big fry pan. It was a real nice homey feeling.

The sound of galloping horse hooves cut through the morning softness like a rusty saw blade. We all stopped and listened in silence at the first sounds, then everyone moved at once. I grabbed the Sharps and ran outside just as I heard Ma scream. I ran around to the back side of the house. When I got there I saw a large black horse running away and a man in the saddle bent low over the woman stretched over the saddle in front of him. Someone had taken Ma.

CHAPTER TWENTY

I panicked. That big black horse looked like the Kid's mount. And now he had Ma. He must have been waiting, watching for his chance. For how long? Had he watched me walk back down the ridge this morning, decided not to shoot me for some reason? Where had he come from? Where was he going?

A thousand questions crowded my mind, but I was already running toward the barn, toward my saddle and my horse. Jim and Shakes were running with me. I reached the barn first.

"Help me saddle," I yelled as they came running in. "Then stay here, protect the place, protect the widow."

They obeyed. It never occurred to me I was this almost sixteen-year-old ordering grown men around, it never occurred to them either. It was just the situation. At certain times we are all grownups and have to act that way. The man with the plan has to speak it out.

My horse was saddled in no time and I rode out of the barn and kicked into a fast trot headed toward the ranch gate and the main road. I looked for fresh sign as I rode along and saw several big hoofprints, newly made. At the gate, I climbed down to take a closer look.

I didn't figure the Kid was staying in town, not with Ike right there. He must have another hideout. I had to be sure which way he went from here. The big hoofprints were headed right toward town. From the look of them, he hadn't even slowed down coming out the ranch gate.

I rode that way at a fast pace but kept an eye along the roadside hoping I'd spot where he turned off, figuring he would. But he didn't, least as far as I could tell. I slowed to a walk on the outskirts of town. The Kline place was dark and still, too early yet for townsfolk to be up, I guessed. I thought I saw a curtain stir on the second floor and a flash of red hair, but maybe I was just hoping.

Once I reached Émile's Blacksmith Shop, I dismounted and led my horse. I checked my loads in the Navy Colt. I smelled bacon and ham and coffee. Someone was having breakfast. A wagon rattled by, a man delivering milk and butter. Other than him, the main street was empty. But somewhere the Kid was watching me, for sure.

When I came to the Deep Water Liberty News office I dismounted and tied the reins to the hitching post. I stepped up on the boardwalk and walked to the open doorway. I knew Ike would be there but didn't know if he'd figured on me. He sat at his desk, his eye on the door as I walked in. He looked at me, waiting.

"The Kid's got Ma," I said.

He stood. The Colt was at his waist, like he was expecting something. He stepped around the desk and took a few steps toward me. No rifle, no shells in the pocket this time. He knew what was coming.

"Where is he?"

"Somewhere in town. He came out to the Box Elder Ranch and took her." I almost teared up right then when I said it, but made it not happen in front of Ike.

That's when we heard the shout out in the street. It was the Kid. There was no mistaking his voice, it had the cold hollowness of the grave in it.

"Ike, come out here. I got the Whittaker woman."

That's all he said. He didn't have to say anything else. Ike brushed past me and went to the door. I came right behind. He stepped to the right of the doorway and I stepped to the left.

The main street of Deep Water ran north and south. There was an alley ran east next to a mercantile building just north of where we stood, across the street from us. The Kid stood there. The Peacemaker sat easy on his right hip, handle out. He was as still as a gravestone.

Ike stepped down into the street. "Where is she, Kid?"

"She's safe, Ike. But you gotta come through me to get to her."

Ike nodded. "I figured."

I walked up the boardwalk to where I was almost across from the Kid. He eyed me, said nothing.

What Ike said next surprised me. "Kid, I don't need her anymore. I got what I needed."

I looked at him, looked back at the Kid. Neither one changed expression. The Kid's face was like a stone slab, nothing there except the two black eyes like twin holes.

Then my eye caught movement beyond Ike. The Lucky 7 Saloon door came open across the street and Will Hanks stepped out on the boardwalk. Casual as a gent taking the air in the park, he stepped down into the street and began to walk toward us.

I tried to figure what he was planning. Did he think he was gonna arrest somebody? Did he want to shoot Ike? The Kid? Ike was between two gunfighters now, Ranger Hanks on one side, the Kid on the other. I had Ike on my right, the Kid across from me, and Ranger Hanks walking toward us making the point of a triangle.

It's funny how your brain slows down to a crawl when things get complicated and dangerous, yet the thoughts keep coming at you like hail stones. Right there in my mind I worked out what likely would happen. Ike knew the Kid wanted to kill him, so he'd try to shoot him first. The Kid was harder to figure. He might be fast enough to try to shoot me first and then Ike, to hurt him just that much more. Or maybe try to wound Ike, put him down, then take on Hanks and shoot me last while Ike could still watch. Was he that quick? I had a suspicion he was.

I should have been scared. I should have been wetting myself by now, but my brain was buzzing with too many possibilities. Ike knew I could shoot, but maybe didn't think I'd shoot him. Ranger Hanks knew I could shoot, he'd watched me practice. But he didn't think I could shoot anything other than a target, was my guess. The

Kid didn't know I could shoot at all. Last time he faced me I was froze up like an icicle.

The other thing I knew about Hanks was how he liked to use opportunity. He wouldn't wait for someone to draw if it didn't suit him, he'd just shoot to kill and explain later. The Kid wouldn't say anything at all. But he was fast, probably thought he was the fastest. He'd likely wait for someone else to draw first and then beat him, just to prove it. I figured Ike for someone to talk first and goad the man into drawing before he was ready.

All this thinking took about two of Ranger Hank's steps coming toward us. I already knew what I had to do.

Ranger Hanks was smiling that smile he wore like he enjoyed his work. He was wearing a badge on his shirt. I drew the Navy, cocking it back as I had practiced for so long and shot Hanks. Right as I did the sun flashed on his badge and made a bright spot, a red spot, just like the spot I'd used for a target. My bullet hit him right there. He was dead before he hit the ground.

I was already cocking back the hammer when my left arm was hit. I knew it was the Kid. But my eyes were on Ike. Even as I shot Hanks, I'd seen Ike draw. I'd never seen anything so smooth and so fast. The Kid's bullet knocked me sideways, but I kept my balance and turned my gun on Ike. After his first shot at the Kid, his Colt was on me. That fast.

But he'd been hit. The Kid's second shot jarred him. Ike's shot clipped my ear. It sounded and felt like a huge bee. My shot put him down. In the same motion I knelt and turned the Navy toward the Kid. He was down on his knees. Ike's shot had been true. The Kid tried to bring his Peacemaker up as I shot him.

I might have imagined it, but the moment before I pulled the trigger one of his black cave eyes seemed to glint like a little red dot. My bullet went right there.

It was over.

134

The gun fight took just a few seconds, but each second was an hour. I pictured every little detail, every movement one after another like watching each car in a slow freight train, one by one. I never heard separate gunshots, just a large echoing noise in the background. I felt the Kid's bullet hit my arm, but not as pain, just a hard punch, just a piece of information to factor in.

Now it was over, I was the only one standing. I was looking at the Kid. I knew he was dead. I turned my head and looked at Ranger Hanks. I knew he was dead, too. My bullet had gone right into his heart. Now I looked at Ike. He was sitting, legs sprawled, looking back at me.

I started toward him. As soon as I moved, pain shot through my left arm. I guessed the Kid's bullet had broken it. I got to Ike, supported his back with my good arm. He groaned.

"Why'd you pull your shot?" I asked. "You had me. You made me shoot you."

There was a rattling in Ike somewhere, then a wheezing. I'd hit him high in the chest. I didn't know where the Kid had hit him.

"I never wanted to hurt you, boy," Ike said. His words was slow and weak. "I always liked you. Like a son."

"There ain't no money, Ike," I said. "What was the point to all this?"

He sagged where I held him, his head sinking. He said a word. I couldn't make it out. I leaned in closer, still holding up his back. He said it again. "Pride."

Then I couldn't hold him anymore and had to lay him out on his back. He looked up at me. Blood flecked his lips. I saw it now in his eyes. Pride. It was for me.

He tried to lift his head. I supported it. "You're better than him," he said. He meant the Kid. Each word came weak, spaced. "You're better than me." He made a choking rattling sound, struggled, spoke one more time. "You're the best I've seen." He relaxed all over, his chest stopped moving. I laid his head back down.

By now people were out in the street. Some stood near Ranger Hanks' body, others stood around the Kid, talkin' quiet, pointing. Mr. Phelps came over to me, looked at Ike and shook his head. Then he saw my arm. "Let me look at that arm, son."

I stood up, pushed him aside. "I got to find Ma," I told him.

I walked past the crowds over to the Lucky 7 Saloon, felt a hand grab my sleeve, pulled away. I walked to the bar and found Bill Spence there. He was getting ready for all the drinks he knew he'd be serving.

"I want the key to Ranger Hanks' room," I said.

He slid it across to me like he knew that's what I'd come for. I walked up the stairs, looked at the key, and went straight to room number three. I unlocked the door, opened it and saw Ma lying on the bed, her hands and feet tied, a bandana shoved in her mouth.

I untied her and she grabbed hold of me tight. I grunted from the pain of my arm and she let me go quick and looked closer. Then she went to the door and called down to Mr. Spence to get the doctor. When she come back, she worked the shirt off me and looked at my arm. There was a pucker hole there, blood oozing. The arm was all black and blue from shoulder to elbow.

She looked at my face, spoke soft. "The others?"

"Dead," I said. "The Kid, Ranger Hanks, Ike—all dead."

She breathed out. "So, it's all over."

"Yeah, Ma, it's all over."

"How did you know where to find me?" Ma asked.

"I always kinda thought the Kid and Ranger Hanks were hooked in this together. Hanks was always the one in charge. I figure Hanks

136

showed the Kid how they both could get what they wanted by teaming up. Why didn't the Kid kill me with all those chances he had? I figure Hanks told him not to until we told him where the money was."

"And Ike?"

I thought about it. "I think Ike was telling the truth. I think he played along with Hanks and his old gang like he said. That was his best chance to protect us. I think maybe when he first came to Deep Water, he did want to find the money, take it all for himself. But after a while he became part of the town, a real citizen, and he kinda liked that. He grew to like you and me, too. I think he changed."

By then I heard boots on the stairs and figured the doctor was on his way up. I was glad because my arm was beginning to hurt like sin. I smiled at Ma. "I think it's like Ike said, the past has a way of never letting go."

CHAPTER TWENTY-TWO

I had killed my best friend. Ike was my friend and my father all rolled into one for the most vulnerable and sensitive time of my life. I come to realize that later. The things he taught me then stuck. They made sense.

Me and Ma were in bad shape for a while following the shooting and all. There was an inquiry a couple of weeks later when the circuit judge came around. He called us all in to testify. Ma and the Widow McKenzie were good witnesses. They told the truth flat and simple. Shakes and Jim told how they'd lost their friend and boss when the Kid hung Tom. Bill Spence had a lot to tell about the connection between Ranger Hanks and Ike's old gang, men like Ewan O'Brien and Weasel Rocco Pernelli. Bill Spence was there when the Kid tried to kill me the first time, back when all the trouble began. Luke the shotgun guard told how he saw Ranger Hanks set up to kill O'Brien. This time the judge believed him.

The only hitch in the giddyap was when Mr. Phelps told the judge how I pulled my gun and shot Ranger Hanks before anyone else pulled theirs. That was a fact I couldn't deny. When the judge called me to the stand, I told them how my thinking went, how I figured each gunfighter was gonna act. There was gonna be a gunfight whether I shot first or last. My decision came down to whether I wanted to be dead or alive.

After a whole lot of back and forth and a long spell of thinking the judge decided I had shot in self-defense. I think the weight of opinion in that courtroom was with me and Ma, for sure. The judge swung his gavel and opened the bar and that was that.

One thing pleased me. Although they found both the Kid and Ranger Hanks guilty of murder the judge found Ike innocent. We buried Ike in the same burying ground as pa. A lot of people came to pray over him. He'd made a lot of friends. It was good to see. The same day, after everyone was gone, I came back and buried the Navy Colt in pa's grave. I wanted the killing part of my life to end right there. I wish I could say it did.

I kept the Bowie knife, though. It was useful around the farm. Every now and again I'd take it out of the leather at night while Ma and I was sitting around the table and shine up the blade and sharpen it if it needed.

One of those times Ma looked at the leather where it lay on the table with the chicken scratch side up. She studied it a bit, then she made a noise and a look of surprise came over her.

"What is it, Ma?"

She looked at me and laughed and said, "I was just casually looking at those markings and of a sudden I recognized them." She laughed again. "Look here." She pointed at the upside-down vees. "These aren't mountain peaks, like I first thought. Sage probably wanted to exaggerate them to look like something else far away. These are hills, the hills right around our farm here. See that?"

Her finger went along the row of vees on the map. Just like she said, the hills that surrounded our place jumped out at me. Now the other markings made sense, one was the house and one was the shed, the circle-like scratch was the fence line.

"Do you think pa actually buried something around here, Ma?" I asked.

"I have no idea. But your pa was, well, unpredictable that way."

We were up bright and early the next morning with the leather scrap and a shovel to follow the trail of arrows to find whatever it was pa had made the map for. The first arrow took us right through the goat pasture and the goats followed us like a crowd of protesters, talkin' the whole way. We slid through the fence at the other side and left them there. The next arrow took us between two of the low hills to the west. The next set of scratches was hard to figure. We studied them and looked around us and finally figured they was meant to be a tree grove down the slope. We went in among the cottonwoods. A small stream, the one that went through the goat pasture gurgled among the trees before going underground.

The final thing etched on the map after that arrow was an eye, looked like. It was an arch over a straight line. We couldn't figure that one, either. We searched the grove real thorough but didn't really know what we expected to find. I was leaning on the shovel and staring at the creek where it went underground, and it come to me. Pa meant it to be a cave. And right where the creek went underground looked like a small cave.

We dug down into the creek bed right there and cut away earth around the top of where it tunneled under and the shovel hit on something solid. We dug out the Wells Fargo box. The lock was missing so we opened it easy and there was stacks of bonds and cash and a fair amount of gold. It was the money, alright. It was a good haul, too, and easy to see why Ranger Hanks and the robbers came to try to find it after all these years.

We couldn't carry it back to the house, so we hitched the horse to a sledge and worked the box onto it and let the horse bring it back for us. At the house we emptied the box bit by bit, moved the box into Ma's bedroom next to pa's storage bin and left it there. I figured we was set for life, but Ma wouldn't have it.

"The money isn't ours to keep," was what she said. "We have to return it."

There was no arguing with her about it. I rode off to Fort Worth where the nearest Wells Fargo office was located to tell them about it. A nice man at a very large wood desk spoke with me and told me how good it was to work with honest citizens and said he'd have to look up the shipment. I waited in the area outside his office on a bench while he looked through ledgers and spoke with clerks about it. After an hour or so he called me in.

"We found the shipment in question," he said. "It is exactly as you describe. It must be pretty near intact. We read the account from the Texas Ranger who pursued the thieves." The man opened a map. "The robbery occurred here." He pointed to a place far south of Fort Worth. "The ranger in his account says he tracked the robbers all the way up here." He pointed to a spot near Deep Water. "He fought them single handed, killed one, captured two, but the leader got away. Now, according to his account he recovered the strongbox, but he couldn't carry it out with him the several days it took to get back to the nearest jail, so he hid it."

I was puzzled. "I always heard he never found the money."

The man looked at me and smiled. "Well, the ranger knew if he told people he found it and buried it, everyone, including the gang leader, would go up there looking for it so he let on like he never recovered it." The man leaned back in his chair. He waved toward the office where the clerks worked. "We were just now trying to understand what happened next. The war began with firing on Fort Sumpter and this state was in turmoil immediately. There were raids down from Indian Territory and up from Mexico. Most of our able men went to join the Confederate Army under Lee. Things got lost in the chaos. If the ranger drew up a map or gave someone directions to recover the strongbox, we can find no record of it. The ranger himself went right off to the war." The man looked at me. "His name was Ranger Sage Whittaker. You said your name was Whittaker. Was he your pa?"

I nodded.

"Well, you come from good stock, I'd say. Anyway, what with the war and all, we have nothing more on that shipment. Meanwhile, we collected insurance on it and forgot about it." He shifted through some papers. "The insurance company, F.F. Rothchild's, put out rewards and finder's fees on it, but of course, no one collected." The man looked at me. "Those rewards are still open. Now what happens in a case like that, inflation kicks in over the years. The sum as it now stands isn't as large as the money and bonds in that box but it's not that far off. You and your ma have a nice large sum of money coming to you."

It turned out just as he said. Wells Fargo sent a special envoy to collect the old box and everything in it. They had us sign a form and sent it on to F.F. Rothchild's. In a month or so, a check arrived in the mail. A very big check. We deposited it right off at Wells Fargo and now they send a check to Ma every month.

With all this you must think we were set to live happily ever after. It should have happened that way, but things never seem to go as you expect in life.

Fact is, word got around, not just about the money Ma and I had found but about the gunfight that came before that. Reporters and writers got hold of it and twisted it and turned the truth to suit themselves, like so often happens. Next you knew, I was a legendary gunfighter. Everyone in town thought that was kinda funny. I guess I did too.

During the year after the gunfight the town figured it should have its own sheriff, so they had Bill Spence sworn in. We had law now. He did a good job of it. When Bill heard the story how I was this great gunfighter he didn't think it was funny. I learned why pretty quick.

CHAPTER TWENTY-THREE

Ma and I tried to settle back into our old routine like it was before the Kid came to town but things was never quite the same. Now that we had money, we spruced the place up a bit. We still kept the goats, but we didn't have to sell any like we did before to make ends meet so we didn't. We bought another horse, a filly just under four years old with lots of spirit. She took to our mare right away and between me and the mare we began teaching her manners.

I began to see something of Meghan once I was brave enough to ask her pa to let me call on her. We'd ride together sometimes, me on the filly and Meghan on our mare. Sometimes we'd ride out to the Box Elder Ranch to see the Widow McKenzie. She'd serve us tea and biscuits and the women would do small talk.

After the gunfight, folks in town were polite to me but standoffish. I didn't pack a handgun since I buried the Navy Colt but even without it, folks seemed wary of me. Awhile after the gunfight, Bill Spence had brought over Ike's Colt Army pistol and belt thinking it fitting I should have it, Ike being like a father to me and all. I put it away in pa's chest. Later I moved it to the newspaper office, which seemed a better place.

I took over the Deep Water Liberty News. I hired an apprentice just like Ike had done me. He was right smart and good at talking to people and learning their stories. My life at sixteen going on seventeen seemed pretty much set.

The thing was, sometimes strangers came to Deep Water talking about the gunfight and asking folks to point me out to them. They'd read some newspaper or magazine story about it more fiction than fact, like as not, and was curious to see where it happened. Bill Spence took to warning me when strangers came to town asking about me and I'd go out the back door of the newspaper and ride home or off somewhere until they got tired of looking and went away. That part of it was a nuisance, but I figured it would fade after a while.

One day a stranger came to town who didn't go away. He hung out at the Lucky 7 Saloon drinking whisky and talking about famous gunfighters and how he was faster. Bill Spence still tended bar even though he was sheriff. He didn't like what he was hearing and came to tell me about it.

"This kind of kid worries me," he said. "He's a lot of mouth and likely not much action but it feels like he's working up to something."

I was close to putting the paper to bed. I was waiting on a news article from my intern and ready to put finishing touches on an editorial. I admit I was impatient with Bill.

"Look, Bill," I said, "I can't stop work for every whisky driven wannabe gunfighter in Texas. Let me just get this paper tucked away and I'll go home. I promise."

Bill went away grumbling about how he didn't know if this drunk kid would keep much longer.

Ten minutes later one of the local cowhands came busting in all worked up. He told me the kid who had been drinking and mouthing off had shot Bill Spence.

I was shocked. "Bill ain't no gun fighter," I said. "He don't even carry a gun."

"The stranger shot him anyway, never mind no gun," the man said. "Now he's struttin' around pointing his pistol every which way and we don't have a sheriff no more."

I walked over to the wall where Ike's Colt and his old rifle still sat. I took down the gun belt and strapped it on. I tossed the rifle to the man and said, "Cover my back."

As I walked down the boardwalk from the newspaper office, I checked the loads in the Colt. It had been a long time since I wore a gun and I never before wore Ike's rig. The man with Ike's rifle followed me a long way behind.

144

I should have known better, I reckon. Here I was thinking this drunk kid would take one look at me packing the Colt and back off. But you can never figure what whiskey will do to a person.

I pushed through the swing doors of the Lucky 7 Saloon and stepped to one side, my eyes going from bright sunlight to dim lamps. First thing I saw was Bill Spence stretched out on the floor. There was people clumped on each side of the room. A man was standing at the bar, his back to me, eyeing a glass of whiskey. He had his hands cupped on each side of the glass like it's the most precious thing in the world. He's wearing a felt hat brown with trail dust, a worn vest, and the ivory grips of two pistols showing each side of him.

I spoke into the silence of the room. "You the one who shot Bill?"

The stranger didn't turn around. He raised the glass, sipped, put it down slow.

"I knew you'd come," he said.

"Take out them pistols with two fingers each hand and drop them to the floor," I said.

"You planning to shoot me in the back?" he asked.

"I ain't planning to shoot you at all, unless you don't do what I tell you."

He didn't move. "You're so almighty fast you won't allow a man a fair fight?"

"This ain't about fighting, this is about arresting," I said.

The stranger laid both hands flat on the counter. "You got a choice to make. You gotta decide to shoot me down or fight fair." He turned around slow now, letting his hands drop.

This was the first I seen him. He looked to be about twenty. He had dark curly hair and a scruff of black whiskers on his face. I expected his eyes to look squirrely, like a man who'd been drinking a while,

145

but they looked clear and steady to me. He took a step toward me away from the bar.

Everything Ike had taught me was in my brain, clear as writing on a chalkboard. First thing was, if I was going to fight the stranger, I was going to kill him. Simple.

Both his pistols were half out of their holsters when my bullet went through his heart.

Turned out Bill Spence had a bullet in his shoulder, and another had grazed his head. The stranger had drawn both guns on an unarmed man. Bill came around after a while and we took him back to his room and laid him on his bed for the doc to work on him. The undertaker took the stranger's body away.

We all tried to get back to business as usual. When the circuit judge came around, he didn't even hold court, enough witnesses said it was self-defense. Now, though, the papers and magazines started up all over again about the gunfighter up in Deep Water.

When Bill Spence told me he'd got a wire from the sheriff in Fort Worth saying the stranger I killed had two brothers and they was coming for me, I knew things would never be the same again. The avengers and the wannabe gunfighters would just keep coming. Bill told me he thought I should leave town for a spell, let things cool down. I knew he was right. But I knew right then I wouldn't ever be back.

I won't tell you about the day I left, about how I told my Ma goodbye, knowing I likely wouldn't ever see her again. I didn't say anything to Meghan. Her pa wouldn't let me see her after I shot the stranger. Maybe he was right about that.

I was the ripe old age of eighteen when I rode away from Deep Water for the last time. I had plenty of time to ponder what brought me to my current circumstances. I suppose I could blame the Kid. It all began when he came to town to feed on revenge.

As I think back now, there were two things Ike used to say always rang true to me in my life. One was you don't always get the chance to be fair. The other was the past don't like to let go of a man.

Other Novels by R Lawson Gamble

ZACK TOLLIVER, FBI series

THE DARK ROAD (prequel)

THE OTHER

MESTACLOCAN

ZACA

CAT

UNDER DESERT SAND

CANAAN'S SECRET

LAS CRUCES

JOHNNY ALIAS series

JOHNNY AND THE PREACHER

Coming Soon
Another R Lawson Gamble Classic Western

JOHNNY AND THE COMMANCHE